The Duke

"Be careful! That bridge is unsafe!"

Startled by the sound, Lynda turned to look round at who had spoken.

As she did so, the bridge rocked and she slipped and fell into the stream.

She had never been taught to swim because her Father considered it not becoming of a young woman.

She gasped for breath, finding it impossible to breathe.

Then she was lifted bodily up onto the grass.

She was aware that a man was standing over her.

It was, in fact, the Duke of Buckington.

"How can you have been such a fool as to try and cross the stream by that bridge?" he demanded.

A Camfield Novel of Love by Barbara Cartland

———

"Barbara Cartland's novels are all distinguished by their intelligence, good sense, and good nature. . . ."
— **ROMANTIC TIMES**

"Who could give better advice on how to keep your romance going strong than the world's most famous romance novelist, Barbara Cartland?"
— **THE STAR**

Camfield Place,
Hatfield
Hertfordshire,
England

Dearest Reader,

Camfield Novels of Love mark a very exciting era of my books with Jove. They have already published nearly two hundred of my titles since they became my first publisher in America, and now all my original paperback romances in the future will be published exclusively by them.

As you already know, Camfield Place in Hertford-shire is my home, which originally existed in 1275, but was rebuilt in 1867 by the grandfather of Beatrix Potter.

It was here in this lovely house, with the best view in the county, that she wrote *The Tale of Peter Rabbit*. Mr. McGregor's garden is exactly as she described it. The door in the wall that the fat little rabbit could not squeeze underneath and the goldfish pool where the white cat sat twitching its tail are still there.

I had Camfield Place blessed when I came here in 1950 and was so happy with my husband until he died, and now with my children and grandchildren, that I know the atmosphere is filled with love and we have all been very lucky.

It is easy here to write of love and I know you will enjoy the Camfield Novels of Love. Their plots are definitely exciting and the covers very romantic. They come to you, like all my books, with love.

Bless you,

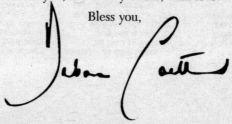

CAMFIELD NOVELS OF LOVE

by Barbara Cartland

A NEW CAMFIELD NOVEL OF LOVE BY

BARBARA CARTLAND

The Duke Finds Love

JOVE BOOKS, NEW YORK

THE DUKE FINDS LOVE

A Jove Book / published by arrangement with
the author

PRINTING HISTORY
Jove edition / May 1994

All rights reserved.
Copyright © 1994 by Barbara Cartland.
Cover art copyright © 1994 by Fiord Forlag A/S.
This book may not be reproduced in whole
or in part, by mimeograph or any other means,
without permission. For information address:
The Berkley Publishing Group, 200 Madison Avenue,
New York, New York 10016.

ISBN: 0-515-11378-6

A JOVE BOOK®
Jove Books are published by The Berkley Publishing Group,
200 Madison Avenue, New York, New York 10016.
JOVE and the "J" design
are trademarks belonging to Jove Publications, Inc.

PRINTED IN THE UNITED STATES OF AMERICA

10 9 8 7 6 5 4 3 2 1

Author's Note

THE splendour of Greece and its brilliance still lights the world.

There would be no Christianity as we know it without the tremendous influence of the Greek Fathers of the Church, who owed their training to Greek Philosophy.

It is only recently that Archaeologists discovered that the images of Buddha in the Far East can be traced back to portraits of Alexander.

The Greek Gods and the enormous effect they had on civilisation still live. We owe to the Greeks the beginning of thought.

The Greeks were never tired of describing light.

They loved the glitter of moist things, stones

and sand washed by the sea, fish churning in the nets.

They spoke of the "rosey-fingered dawn," when the whole body of Apollo poured across the sky, flashing with a million points of light, germinating the seeds, and defying the powers of darkness.

He was the stars and the Milky Way, the sparkle of the waves and the gleam in the eyes of those who love each other.

His constant companion was the dolphin, the sleekest and shiniest of all living creatures.

When Homer described the goddess Athene, he called her the "Bright-Eyed One."

To him, as for the Greeks, almost everything that was shining was holy.

For them the Goddess of Love was not a many-breasted matron, but a young virgin arising out of the waves.

To them virginity was fresh, clean, and full of promise, like the coming of each day.

It is this purity which is needed at the moment in the world, and I cannot help feeling that only the light of the Divine Radiance will bring it back.

We need the cleanness of Greek thinking away from the filth and perversion that has grown up so rapidly in the last fifteen years.

Ibn Khaldun, the great Arab Philosopher, set out to study the rise and fall of civilisation.

He said that they acted in the same way, obeying ineluctable laws.

He also said it sometimes happened that civilisation would come into existence as a result of a Divine visitation.

It is a Divine visitation that occurred in Greece.

Suddenly the sky seemed brighter, the earth more beautiful, and men's minds moved faster.

Their bodies were equipped with unsuspected powers.

It was as though all the long years of nightmare were over and they came into the clear light of day.

"Where others see but the dawn coming over the hill," says Blake, "I see the sons of God shouting for joy."

That is how the Greeks regarded themselves, and it is what we must look for and pray for in our own world at this moment.

chapter one

1870

LADY Lynda walked out through the front-door and across the garden.

She was singing in her heart because she was home.

It was Spring and everything was bursting into bud.

She had been away for over a year and she thought nothing could be more wonderful than England in May.

She had been abroad at a Finishing School.

She had enjoyed learning, and visiting the marvellous Museums that were available in France.

At the back of her mind, however, there had always been England, its woods, its lakes, its streams and, most of all, her own home.

Marlowe Castle was very old.

She was well aware that, because her Father, the Duke, was not rich, it needed a great many repairs.

But to her, every stone of it was precious.

Not even the creaking floorboards and the damp ceilings could change her love of it.

As she walked into the Park and started to move under the great oak trees, she was thinking of how much she would miss her Mother.

She realised that everything would be different now that she was dead.

Lady Lynda should have been presented to the Queen last year at Buckingham Palace.

She had been nearly eighteen and an important *débutante* of the Season.

Yet when the Duchess of Marlowe died, she chose to remain at School, even though she was older than most of the other girls.

There was a great deal more she wanted to study.

She continued her lessons with the elderly Tutors and spent a lot of time at the various Libraries in Paris.

They were made available to students who were in the top form.

"You will become so clever, Lynda," the other girls warned her, "that every man you meet will be afraid of you."

"I shall be much more afraid of being bored by them," Lynda retorted, "and from what you have all told me, most men have no interest beyond sport."

The girls laughed at her.

Her French friends talked incessantly of how their brothers pursued the attractive, sophisticated women of Paris.

Their English counterparts, however, appeared to have no other interests apart from horses and game-shooting.

"In the Autumn," Lynda's English friends would say, "they go first to Scotland to shoot grouse. Then they come home, where they shoot pheasants and partridge."

"After that they hunt, unless the ground is too frosty. Then when the New Year starts, it is racing, racing, on some Course every week."

Lady Lynda enjoyed riding and insisted on doing so even when she was at School.

At the same time, she found a great number of other things, even more entrancing, to do.

She read about the countries of the world in books.

She studied their customs and traditions as well as learning their languages from her friends.

She thought that if she ever had the opportunity of going to foreign countries, she would be able to converse with their inhabitants.

"You are never likely to go to any outstanding place," she was told.

But she felt in her heart that one day it was what she would do.

The customs of the countries she read about were as vividly imprinted in her mind as were her own.

She had arrived back from France late last night and found, as she might have expected, that her Father had a house-party.

It was the servants who told her that a Steeple-Chase had taken place that day.

A great number of the competitors were staying at the Castle.

Mrs. Meadows, the Housekeeper, who had loved Lynda ever since she was a child, had given her a list of the guests.

She ran her finger down it and realised that most of the names were familiar to her.

She had heard her Father talking about them ever since she was small because they were race-horse owners.

Some of the younger men she could remember competing in the Point-to-Points which her Father arranged as well as the Steeple-Chases.

She admired them, but as she had been so young, she could only peep at them through the bannisters or watch them from the Minstrels' Gallery above the Banqueting Hall as they dined.

They had sometimes talked to her when she was watching the Point-to-Point.

But she was considered too young to ride with them in the morning, which she resented.

4

"You will have the opportunity of meeting plenty of gentlemen when you become a *débutante*," her Mother had said, "and I think it a great mistake for a young girl of fifteen or sixteen, when they are still in the School-Room, to be with older men."

Lynda had to be content with that.

Now, looking down the list which Mrs. Meadows had brought her, she saw one name which she recognised rather better than the others.

"So the Duke of Buckington is here," she said aloud.

"Oh, yes, M'Lady," Mrs. Meadows replied. "His Grace was delighted to have him taking part in the Steeple-Chase."

"Did he win?" Lynda questioned.

"As might have been expected, M'Lady, he won, and a lot of people said it wasn't fair, as he had the best horses and there was really no point in competing against them!"

Lynda was listening.

Yet she was really thinking of what one of her friends at School had told her about the Duke.

Alice Dalton was the daughter of one of the great Beauties of London.

Lynda realised that Lady Dalton had little time for her daughter, who was nearly as beautiful as she was.

She much preferred her son.

She had sent Alice to the School in France,

where Lynda was, simply to get rid of her.

A girl of sixteen betrayed her own age in a way that she considered was definitely to her disadvantage.

Lady Dalton had been a reigning Beauty in London Society for some years.

She had no intention, if she could help it, of giving up her throne.

She admitted reluctantly to being thirty.

She was well aware, when the gossips looked at Alice, that there was a quizzical expression in their eyes which told her that they did not believe her.

Alice, therefore, was posted off to France.

She was told that whenever it was possible during the School holidays, she would stay with friends.

Lynda felt sorry for Alice, aware in contrast how fond her Father and Mother were of her.

She therefore tried to make Alice interested in some of the things which enthralled her.

It was difficult, because Alice wanted to talk about her Mother, and inevitably of the men who pursued her.

Among them was the handsome, dashing, and socially important Duke of Buckington.

"Mama is crazy about him!" she told Lynda. "But although he spends a lot of time with her, I have been told there are a number of other women in his life."

Lynda had at first not understood exactly what Alice was implying.

Finally, she realised that Lady Dalton was being unfaithful to her husband and was extremely shocked.

She did not say so to Alice.

She thought about it for quite a long time, then was aware that it was something that happened frequently in the history books she read.

But she had not, and she thought it stupid of her, expected the behaviour of Kings and Princes to be repeated in what she thought of as a much more enlightened civilisation.

Apparently the behaviour of Charles II with Lady Castlemaine and other ladies of his Court still went on among the dashing young men in present-day Society, like the Duke of Buckington.

She had read about the Regency Bucks and *Beaux*.

Of George IV's infatuation, first with Mrs. Fitzherbert, whom he was secretly supposed to have married, and then his attraction to a number of much older women than himself, like the Marchioness of Hertford and Lady Conyngham.

Lynda thought of how much her Mother loved her Father and how he adored her.

It was impossible to imagine either of them being interested, if that was the right word, in anybody else.

According to Alice, the Duke had captured her Mother's heart.

She was not only in love with him, but also desperately jealous of any other woman with whom he spent his time.

'It may be disgraceful of Lady Dalton,' Lynda ruminated to herself, 'but it is despicable of a gentleman to seduce a married woman, and for her children, like Alice, to know about it.'

She had tried not to think of the depths of depravity to which the Duke and Lady Dalton had sunk.

But Alice would talk:

"The Duke comes to the house when Papa is away. I hear him going upstairs to Mama's bedroom after dinner. At dawn I hear him creeping down and letting himself out through the front-door."

"I do not believe that!" Lynda said. "You are making it up! You would surely be asleep when dawn breaks."

"Sometimes I am awake," Alice argued. "I hear him closing the front-door behind him and going down the street. When Papa is away, Mama always tells the Night-footman there is no need for him to be on duty in the hall."

Lynda had been at home a year ago, just before her Mother died.

Her Father had held a Point-to-Point at Marlowe Castle and the Duke had been one of the competitors.

Lynda could not help looking at him curiously, remembering all she had heard about him.

It was then only the beginning of his *liaison*

amoureuse, as the French called it, with Lady Dalton.

Lynda had been deeply shocked.

Even more so when Alice told her that he had been talked about the previous year with an attractive Lady-in-Waiting to Queen Victoria.

"Does every woman in the Social World betray her husband?" Lynda had asked herself.

When she had seen the Duke, however, she could understand in a way why women found him so attractive.

Tall with broad shoulders, and handsome, he cut a dashing figure and was certainly an outstanding rider.

He won the Point-to-Point by only a length through sheer expertise.

The man he had beaten was furious.

"Dammit, Buck!" Lynda heard him say furiously, as they pulled in their horses. "You have taken my wife from me, that Soiled Dove I fancied, and now, curse you, one-thousand pounds for winning the race!"

Because he was so angry his voice rang out.

It was impossible for Lynda to misunderstand what he was saying.

The Duke, however, had merely laughed.

"I am sorry, Edward," he said, "but if you like, I will toss you for it, double or quits!"

"With your luck," the man called Edward replied, "I would be an utter fool to challenge you. But one day, mark my words, one day you will get your just deserts. Make no mistake about it!"

With that, he rode away, muttering to himself as he did so.

The Duke had seemed quite unperturbed.

He patted his horse approvingly before trotting off.

The crowd and the Duke of Marlowe were waiting to applaud him.

'Poor Alice,' Lynda thought, knowing she was another sufferer at the hands of the victorious Duke.

She had not met him on that visit.

Her Mother had kept her firmly in the School-Room although she had peeped at the guests as they dined.

She would watch them from the windows as they rode in the Park, but had not come into contact with them.

'Now I shall meet the Duke,' she thought.

She wished she could tell him how appalled she was by his behaviour and how much Alice Dalton was suffering because of him.

She had clung to Lynda when she was leaving the School.

"You are going back to England," she said, "but Mama says that, as no-one has asked me to stay this holiday, I am to remain here."

She paused and then continued:

"She does not wish to see me, or, rather, she does not want the Duke or any of her other men-friends who admire her to even be aware of my existence."

Alice had burst into tears before she continued:

"What is to . . . happen next . . . year when I am to be . . . presented?"

"I am sure your Mother will accept the situation by then," Lynda said in an effort to comfort her friend.

"It is the Duke—I am sure it is because of the Duke! She is afraid he will not love her any more once he knows she is not as young as she pretends to be."

"How old is he?" Lynda asked.

"He is twenty-eight, and, if I was born in 1852, as Papa says I was, that makes her at least thirty-five."

Lynda thought privately that it was impossible for Lady Dalton to keep up the pretence for long.

At the same time, all the other girls had gone home to their parents.

But Alice had to stay at School with only one of the older teachers to keep her company.

"I will tell you what I will do," Lynda said. "I will ask Papa if you can come and stay with me, but I have to find out first whether he intends to take me to London to be presented."

She paused and then continued:

"It is only a question of my staying with one of my relations when I go to Buckingham Palace, then I am sure he will agree to have you with us when we are in the country."

"I would love that!" Alice said. "Oh, please, Lynda, do try to have me."

"Of course I will," Lynda said. "And do not be too unhappy."

"How can I be anything else," Alice asked miserably, "when Mama does not want me and Papa is interested only in teaching the boys how to shoot. He takes no interest in any of the things that interest me."

There was nothing Lynda could say.

She could only kiss Alice and promise she would write to her as soon as she reached England.

She was, however, determined to talk to her Father as soon as the house-party was over.

He had come to her after she was in bed and kissed her affectionately.

"I am sorry, my Dearest," he said, "that you arrived too late for the Point-to-Point."

"I could not come earlier, Papa," Lynda explained, "because there were so many people in France to whom I had to say good-bye and to thank for their kindness to me."

The Duke had looked at her questioningly, and she went on:

"I have not been moving in French Society, but I have been taught and helped by a great number of extremely intelligent Professors."

She smiled and then said:

"So I had to thank them for their kindness to an English girl who asked too many questions!"

The Duke laughed.

"At least you are home now," he said, "and it is delightful to have you back, my precious daughter."

He bent and kissed her, then went back downstairs to his party.

*   *   *

Because it had been a very tiring journey, Lynda slept late, although she had meant to ride before breakfast.

Mrs. Meadows brought her breakfast to her bed-side.

When she got up, she decided it would be a mistake to ride alone.

It might upset her Father.

Instead, she would go out with the party after luncheon.

It was usual for the women guests at the Marlowe Castle house-parties to attend Church on Sundays if they wished to.

But on Sunday mornings the men usually rode.

In the afternoon the whole party invariably took carriages, or some went on horseback, up to the Folly.

It was on high ground at the back of the Castle.

From it, there was a magnificent view looking, as the Duke always said proudly, over three different Counties.

It was certainly an interesting way of entertaining his guests.

They then returned to the Castle to a sumptuous tea.

The ladies always rested before dinner.

It was all so familiar; Lynda knew the programme by heart.

In the past, however, she had played very little part in it, except that she went with her Mother to Church.

Now, she thought, she would take her Mother's place.

There was an ache in her heart as she thought of how much she would miss her.

Every room, every piece of furniture, every picture and ornament, reminded her of how happy they had all been since she was a child.

It had been a bitter disappointment to the Duke that his wife, whom he adored, had not been able to have any more children after Lynda was born.

He became so fond of her that it made up for the sadness of not being able to have a son to inherit the title.

The Castle had been in the family for five-hundred years and the Duke still dreamt that one day he would be able to repair it.

He wanted to put back the moat which had gradually dried out and grown over in the passing centuries.

He wanted to make his home as it had once

been, one of the great, outstanding Castles of England.

Lynda walked under the oak trees and across a flat piece of land which led down to the stream, dividing the parkland from the woods. She loved the woods best of all, three-thousand acres which belonged to her Father.

From the time she had been small and her Mother had read her Fairy Stories, she had been certain there were elves and goblins under the trees.

There were fairies fluttering over the bluebells in the Spring.

Nymphs lay deep beneath the still waters of the forest pool which was surrounded with kingcups.

The stories her Mother had read to her had seemed very real.

They repeated themselves from the moment she went under the branches of the oaks and elms, and also when she saw the beauty of the silver birches against the darkness of the firs.

She found herself hurrying until she reached the bridge which spanned the stream.

She was impatient to be in the woods that always meant so much to her.

She felt that they, too, were waiting impatiently for her return.

Then, as she reached the bridge, she stopped.

The rains, which her Father had told her in a letter had been very severe during April, had raised the level of the stream.

Usually it was narrow, and the wooden bridge was high above the water.

Now Lynda saw that the stream had risen until it touched the bridge.

It appeared to be soaked where the water had flooded against its sides.

Nothing, however, was going to deter her from reaching the fairy-tale wood.

The bridge had no hand rail on which to cling.

Knowing the planks would be slippery, Lynda stepped onto it carefully.

She felt the wood creaking beneath her as she gingerly placed one foot in front of the other.

She had reached the centre of the bridge when she heard the sound of horse's hooves.

Then a man's voice behind her shouted:

"Be careful! That bridge is unsafe!"

Because she was startled by the sound, Lynda turned to look round at who had spoken.

As she did so, the bridge rocked and she slipped and fell into the stream.

Struggling to save herself, she realised that at its centre the stream was very deep.

She felt herself sinking.

As the water closed over her head, she was still struggling frantically.

She had never been taught to swim because her Father considered it was not becoming of a young woman.

It flashed through her mind that she would

drown unless somebody came to her assistance.

She gasped for breath, then gasped again, finding it impossible to breathe.

Then someone caught hold of her and dragged her by the neck of her gown up into the air.

Spluttering and gasping, Lynda found herself dragged to the side of the stream.

Then she was lifted bodily up onto the grass.

She was half stifled by the water she had swallowed, which had prevented her from breathing.

It therefore took her a little time before she tried to wipe her eyes.

This she did with the back of her hand.

Then someone put a damp handkerchief into one of them.

She found it easier with that, and at last she opened her eyes.

She was aware that a man was standing over her, as wet as she was.

His horse was cropping the grass behind him.

It took her a second or two to realise that she had seen the man before.

It was, in fact, the Duke of Buckington.

"How can you have been such a fool as to try and cross the stream by that bridge?" he demanded. "It is not only slippery, but also broken!"

"I . . . I did not . . . know it was . . . b-broken," Lynda managed to gasp, "but . . . thank you . . . thank you . . . for . . . saving . . . me."

"At the cost of a good suit!" the Duke replied.

He tried to wring some of the water out of the corner of his riding-coat, then gave up.

Taking off the coat, he flung it down on the ground.

"The best thing we can do," he said, "is to get back to the Castle as quickly as possible and change our clothes."

He spoke indifferently, as if he were thinking of himself rather than of Lynda.

Then, as an afterthought, he asked:

"I suppose you are staying in the Castle?"

"I live there," Lynda said coldly.

She had managed to sit up by this time and was aware that she was soaked to the skin.

Her hair was wet and her slippers had been lost as she struggled in the water.

"I think I know who you are!" the Duke said. "You are my host's daughter. He told me you had arrived late last night."

"That is right," Lynda confirmed, "and I was too late to see the Point-to-Point."

She rose to her feet as she spoke.

As if the Duke were suddenly aware that she had no shoes on her feet, he said:

"You had better ride back on *Rufus*. I will walk."

He did not wait for her to agree, but picked her up in his arms and set her on the saddle.

Taking the bridle, he started to lead the horse back across the flat land towards the Park.

"You have left your . . . coat behind," Lynda reminded him.

"I will send my Valet to pick it up," he answered.

The Duke spoke in a harsh tone of voice.

It told Lynda that he was extremely annoyed at having to rescue her and getting wet in the process.

She was feeling very dishevelled and also somewhat humiliated.

"How," she asked herself, "could I have been aware that the bridge was broken?"

She resented the fact that the Duke thought she was stupid to have walked across it when it was wet.

It was something she had often done in the past.

In fact, she had crossed to the wood when the bridge was thick with snow, or shining with frost.

There had never been a time when it had not carried her from one back to the other.

Knowing how much she loved going into the wood, she thought her Father would have seen to it that the bridge was repaired.

Because she was curious, she asked the Duke:

"How did you know that the bridge was broken?"

"When we were riding here yesterday on our way to the Point-to-Point," he explained, "I noticed that the water was passing over it on the other bank, and pointed it out to your Father."

The way the Duke spoke told Lynda he considered her very unobservant.

She should have seen what was wrong before she attempted to cross the stream.

She admitted to herself that she had been so lost in her eagerness to reach the wood that she had not thought to inspect her surroundings. She'd been dreaming of the stories she would tell herself once she was under the trees.

It had never occurred to her that the passage might be difficult.

The Duke was walking very quickly, as if to offset the discomfort of his wet clothes.

She noticed that his shoulders were very broad and that his waist was slim, tapering down to narrow hips.

It struck her that his was the ideal body of a Greek God.

Then she told herself indignantly that she would never compare the Duke, whom she despised, with the Gods who came from Olympus.

Because she had read so much about them, they were more important to her than any living man.

'There are plenty of people to admire him,' she thought bitterly, 'but he never gives a thought for those he hurts and injures by his bad behaviour!'

It took them nearly a quarter-of-an-hour to walk through the Park.

They crossed the bridge over what had once

been the moat and reached the Court-yard.

As they did so, Lynda was aware that the other guests who had been riding—about six men and two women—had just returned.

They were dismounting in front of the steps which led up to the front-door.

As the Duke appeared, leading his horse with Lynda sitting in the saddle, they stared in astonishment.

Then one of the men exclaimed:

"Good Lord, Buck! What have you been up to now?"

"Rescuing a damsel in distress!" the Duke answered. "She fell into the stream and I was obliged to play the Knight-errant and pull her out!"

He spoke in a disdainful manner which made it clear that he despised her stupidity.

Lynda blushed.

"You certainly look a mess!" one of the other men exclaimed.

Then a woman who had just dismounted and had one foot on the steps turned round to say:

"But—how romantic! Trust Buck to behave like a hero and have us all acclaiming him!"

There was no doubt she was being spiteful.

With an affected laugh she added:

"And how very clever of you, Dear Buck, to find such a pretty girl to rescue!"

With that she walked up the steps.

Two of the men laughed, then one of them said:

"What you need, Buck, is a strong drink and a hot bath."

The Duke did not answer.

He had taken his horse to the steps and now he reached up and lifted Lynda down.

She would have preferred to get down herself, but her gown seemed to stick to the saddle.

Therefore she could not prevent him from helping her.

"Thank you," she said.

She ran up the steps as the men started to ask the Duke exactly what had happened.

The old Butler exclaimed in consternation when Lynda entered the hall.

"Send a housemaid to me!" Lynda ordered.

Her gown was wet, and she found it difficult to climb the stairs quickly, as it was clinging to her legs.

She wanted to run, she wanted to get away from the Duke and the men who were laughing at him.

She wanted also to run away from her own feelings of discomfort and humiliation.

"How could I have been so stupid on my first day at home?" she asked as she entered her bedroom.

As she pulled off her wet clothes she thought how much she disliked the Duke.

It was extremely annoying to be beholden to him.

chapter two

MRS. Meadows helped Lynda to undress and insisted that she should get into bed.

"You've had a shock, M'Lady," she said, "and when anything like that happens, you have to rest."

Because Lynda had no wish to go down to luncheon and explain in detail what had happened, she obeyed Mrs. Meadows.

A delicious meal was brought up to her, but she felt sick.

It was, she knew, the amount of water she had swallowed.

So she only toyed with the dishes the Chef had produced.

Afterwards she fell asleep.

*　　*　　*

When Lynda awoke it was tea-time.

"I will go down to dinner," she told herself.

She knew she ought to support her Father as her Mother had done.

She had, however, learnt from Mrs. Meadows that one of her Father's relatives was in the house.

Lady Hillebrough had last night acted as hostess at the dinner-party and again at luncheon.

"I believe Her Ladyship's leaving after tea," Mrs. Meadows said, "so His Grace'll want you now you're home, to sit at the top of the table."

She paused before she added:

"And very pretty you'll look! We've been saying downstairs that you've grown more like your Mother in the last year and nobody could deny that she was a beauty from the top of her head to the soles of her feet!"

"She was indeed," Lynda agreed softly. "How I wish she were here!"

She said the last words unhappily.

She did not want Mrs. Meadows to go on talking about her Mother.

It was impossible to prevent the tears from coming into her eyes.

It was different at School, where they had not met her Mother.

Here everybody had lived with her and loved

her, and it was difficult not to cry once again at her loss.

Lynda was rested and had no idea what was going on below.

The party had come back from seeing the Folly and eaten a large tea.

It was then that Lady Hillebrough, the Duke's Cousin, told him she wanted to speak to him.

The Duke took her into the Study, and when he had shut the door he said:

"I am sorry you have to leave, Edith, but thank you very much for coming to my assistance."

"I have enjoyed it," Lady Hillebrough assured him, "but what I want to talk to you about, Arthur, is Lynda."

"She is all right after her ducking?" the Duke asked anxiously.

"I believe so," Lady Hillebrough replied, "but I did not go and see her because Mrs. Meadows said she was asleep. She will soon recover, although being nearly drowned is upsetting, to say the least of it."

"I am extremely grateful to Buckington for saving her," the Duke remarked.

"That is what I wanted to speak to you about," Lady Hillebrough said.

The Duke raised his eyebrows, but he did not speak and after a moment his Cousin went on:

"The fact that he saved her from drowning has naturally caused a sensation amongst your party, and I am very much afraid that when they gossip about it in London, it will hurt Lynda's reputation."

The Duke frowned.

"Are you sure about that?"

"The Countess of Eversham, who I think is an extremely spiteful woman, made it clear what she thought about it."

The Duke's frown deepened.

He had never liked the Countess of Eversham, although her husband was a particularly fine rider.

It was impossible to prevent the Earl from joining in the Point-to-Point.

"The Countess, unfortunately," Lady Hillebrough went on, "has the ear of Her Majesty, and you know how particular the Queen is that young girls should behave themselves and not in any way be gossiped about before they are married."

She paused and then continued:

"I think, Arthur, you should speak to the Duke of Buckington."

There was silence until the Duke of Marlowe said in an incredulous tone:

"Are you suggesting, Edith, that I should tell him to make amends for what might appear as an indiscretion?"

"That is exactly what I am saying," Lady Hillebrough replied, "and of course, as a man of the world, he will know that it is his duty."

She glanced at the clock and said:

"Now I must go. It is unfortunate that I cannot stay longer, but George arranged a dinner-party and it is impossible for me not to be there."

"Of course, of course," the Duke agreed, "and as I have said before, Edith, I am very grateful to you."

He walked with her to the front-door, and waited until she had driven away.

Then he said to the Butler:

"Ask His Grace, the Duke of Buckington, to come to my Study. You will find him, I think, in the Billiard Room."

The Butler bowed and hurried away.

The Duke went back to his Study.

He had to wait for about ten minutes before the Duke of Buckington appeared.

He walked into the room looking extremely elegant, wearing the clothes in which he had driven a Four-in-Hand up to the Folly.

The Duke of Marlowe had been well aware that he would enjoy handling that particular team.

"You wanted me, Marlowe?" he asked.

"Yes," the Duke replied, "I wanted to talk to you, Buck. Sit down and have a glass of champagne."

"Thank you," the Duke of Buckington replied. "I have earned it! I have just beaten Harry by one point at the Billiard table, and you know that he is at the moment the champion of White's Club."

The Duke of Marlowe poured out a glass of champagne from the bottle that stood on the grog-tray in a corner of the room.

He handed it to his guest before going back to pour out a glass for himself.

Standing with his back to the fireplace, he said slowly:

"First, I must thank you for saving my daughter's life. It was very remiss of me not to inform her that the bridge over the stream was broken, but I was not expecting her to want to go there immediately after her return."

"You should have taught her to swim," the Duke remarked lightly. "It is something everybody learns to do at School, but it is supposed to be indecent for a young woman."

He laughed as he spoke, but the Duke of Marlowe was looking serious.

"It was extremely resourceful of you to rescue her like that," he said, "and of course in keeping with your reputation."

"It was fortunate that I was there," the Duke of Buckington replied. "I had left those who were riding with me because I remembered that I had written a very important letter this morning to the Manager of my race-horses and had forgotten to hand it to one of your servants for posting."

The Duke nodded, and he went on:

"You may be interested to know what it contains! I am bidding for Franklin's six horses that are coming up at Tattersalls Salesrooms on Tuesday."

The Duke of Marlowe sighed.

"I envy you," he said, "I would like to have those horses myself, but I cannot afford them."

"I am afraid they are going to cost me a pretty penny!" the Duke of Buckington said. "But they are exceptionally fine, and perhaps one of them will win the Derby."

"If you enter any of them, I shall certainly back him," the Duke of Marlowe remarked.

There was silence until he went on:

"Why I asked you to come here, Buck," he said, "is that my Cousin, Lady Hillebrough, whom you met last night, told me before she left just now that she is exceedingly perturbed by your gallantry where my daughter Lynda is concerned."

The Duke raised his eyebrows.

"You mean I upset her?" he asked.

"No, no, not that," the Duke of Marlowe replied. "My Cousin is thinking of her reputation, and apparently the Countess of Eversham is already making something of a song and dance about it!"

The Duke of Buckington's lips tightened.

He knew exactly why the Countess was being unpleasant where he was concerned.

She had stalked him as if he were a stag for nearly six months.

She gave up only when she realised that he had no intention of responding to her advance.

Although she was acclaimed a Beauty, he was not one of her admirers.

In fact, he found her sharp tongue unpleasant and her type of beauty left him cold.

Aloud he said:

"I should not worry about anything Margaret Eversham says. If she ever said a kind word, it was a mistake."

The Duke of Marlowe gave a short laugh before replying:

"Unfortunately, as we both know, the Countess has the ear of the Queen. I do not wish my daughter's reputation to be damaged before she even makes her curtsy at Buckingham Palace."

He spoke slowly and pompously.

As if it suddenly dawned on the Duke of Buckington exactly what this conversation was leading up to, he sat upright in his chair.

"You're not suggesting, Marlowe . . . ?" he asked.

"I think you understand," the Duke interrupted, "that I have first and foremost to think of my daughter. She is, as you know, my only child, and very precious to me."

The Duke of Buckington drew in his breath and put down his glass.

Rising from the chair in which he was sitting, he walked to the window.

He stood looking out with unseeing eyes at the sunset.

Then, in a voice that hardly sounded like his own, he said:

"You are asking too much, Marlowe."

"I am asking you to behave like a Gentleman!" the Duke retorted.

There was silence until the Duke of Buckington said, almost as if he were speaking to himself:

"I have no intention of getting married for at least another ten years."

"I can understand that," the Duke of Marlowe replied, "but I have to think of my daughter."

Again there was silence, and the very air in the room seemed to vibrate between the two men.

Then, as if the Duke of Buckington realised there was nothing he could do, he said harshly:

"Very well, Marlowe, I will marry your daughter, but God knows what sort of husband I will make for an unfledged girl!"

He did not wait for the Duke to reply, but turned and walked out of the Study.

* * *

He did not shut the door, but left it ajar.

The Duke of Marlowe heard his footsteps going down the passage towards the hall.

The Duke gave a deep sigh that was one of relief.

He knew Buckington, of all men, had no wish to marry.

He had never been known to have anything to do with young girls.

They were paraded before him by their ambitious Mamas like horses at a Spring Fair.

The Duke told himself, however, that there was nothing else he could have done in the circumstances.

It was unfortunate for Buckington that it had been he who had rescued Lynda from drowning.

Had it been anybody else in the house-party, it could have been glossed over, or else, just been laughed about for a short time until it was forgotten.

The Duke of Buckington had been the greatest matrimonial catch not only of this Season, but of every Season since he had come into the title.

The Duke knew there was not a family in England who would not welcome him as a son-in-law.

His magnificent houses and his huge fortune were only a background to the man himself.

He had been admired, talked about, and envied ever since he had become of importance in the Social World.

Looking back, the Duke could not remember any speculation about whom he should marry.

What was said of him concerned his numerous love-affairs which kept the gossips' tongues wagging from January to December.

At the same time, he excelled in the field of sport.

There was not a man of consequence who did not try to emulate him.

The Duke had known that it was the sportsman in him that made Buckington agree to his behest.

A lesser man might have crept away from the mess into which he had unintentionally fallen.

'It is bad luck for Buckington,' the Duke of Marlowe thought, 'at the same time, it is an ill wind which blows nobody any good.'

He was thinking as he spoke how extremely advantageous it was for him to have the Duke as his son-in-law at this particular moment.

To do him credit, it had not occurred to the Duke of Marlowe until now what a difference Lynda's marriage could make to him personally.

Now he realised the enormity of it.

He was suddenly aware that the whole world seemed brighter than it had for some time.

He glanced at the clock and realised it was time to dress for dinner.

He wondered if he should stop on his way to his room to speak to Lynda.

Then he told himself that would be a mistake.

Buckington would be leaving to-morrow morning.

Doubtless he would wish to propose to Lynda in his own way before he left.

*   *   *

When Lynda was ready to join the house-party, she found them gathered in the Drawing-Room.

As she came into the room, she looked very attractive in a white gown which she had bought in Paris.

There was, however, not admiration but a look of curiosity in everyone's eyes.

"You are all right now, I hope?" one of the ladies asked. "We have been worried about you. It must have been a tremendous shock."

"I am quite all right, thank you," Lynda replied.

"You certainly timed your accident at exactly the right moment!" the Countess of Eversham remarked. "How very fortunate that Buck was passing at that particular instant! Or perhaps there was an assignation between you two young people?"

She was obviously being spiteful, and Lynda thought it best not to answer.

Instead, she went up to one of her Father's men-friends and said:

"Do tell me how your horses did yesterday in the Point-to-Point. I was so disappointed to have missed it."

Because she had avoided answering the Countess of Eversham's pertinent question, several of the house-party exchanged glances.

It was at that moment that the Duke of

Marlowe came into the room.

"You must forgive me for being late," he said, "but I forgot the time."

"That is an excuse which has been used a thousand times," one of the men remarked, "and there is usually a very good reason for it!"

"And of course, a pretty one!" another man chipped in.

They were laughing, but the Duke of Marlowe did not join in.

It had suddenly struck him that the Duke of Buckington might leave the Castle rather than face the music.

It was, therefore, with a sense of relief that he saw that the Duke of Buckington was the next person to come into the room:

"My apologies for being late," he said to the Duke of Marlowe.

"I thought perhaps you had gone for another swim," someone remarked.

The Duke did not make a response, and the joke fell flat.

When dinner was announced, the Duke of Marlowe offered his arm to the Countess of Eversham.

"Your pretty daughter appears none the worse after her dramatic episode," the Countess said as they walked down the corridor. "Was it really an accident, or do you think it was a new way of meeting in secret?"

She laughed, but the Duke was scowling as they entered the Dining-Room.

Lynda had already been told by Mrs. Meadows that she was to sit in her Mother's place at the top of the table.

She was relieved to find that it was not the Duke of Buckington who was seated on her right; on both sides of her were two elderly gentlemen.

She found it easy to talk to them.

When the ladies had left the Dining-Room, they each told the Duke of Marlowe how charming they found his daughter.

"You must be glad to have her home, Arthur," one of them said.

Before the Duke could reply, the other man said:

"Considering how attractive she is, I do not suppose it will be for long!"

The Duke glanced at the Duke of Buckington, who could not help overhearing what had been said.

He was aware that his future son-in-law was looking annoyed and quickly changed the subject.

When the gentlemen joined the ladies, a number of the guests went into the Card-Room and sat down to play Whist.

Four of the men went to the Billiard-Room.

As the Duke of Marlowe had hoped, the Duke of Buckington and Lynda were now alone.

It seemed as if Fate were playing into his hands, and it was up to him to take the initiative.

He said:

"I think, Lynda, that the Duke has something to say to you. Perhaps it would be better if you went into the Music-Room, where you will not be disturbed."

Lynda looked surprised.

Then she thought her Father was giving her the opportunity to thank the Duke for saving her life.

It was something she could quite easily do where they were, but there was no point in arguing.

She, therefore, led the way from the room and along the corridor to the Music-Room.

It was a very attractive room, or would have been if it had not needed repair.

The walls certainly required repainting, and the curtains were faded and torn.

There was, however, a grand piano on which her Mother had played to Lynda ever since she had been a child.

She herself was quite an accomplished pianist, having had an excellent teacher when she was at School.

The minute she entered the room she saw that the plants which filled the fireplace when there was no fire needed renewing.

There was a large arrangement of tulips and daffodils on the piano that were almost dead.

Then, as the Duke shut the door, Lynda said quickly:

"I cannot think why Papa sent us here,

except, of course, that I wanted to thank you most sincerely for rescuing me this afternoon."

She paused and then continued:

"Papa said he knew the bridge was broken, but had not expected me to go to the woods so soon after my return from France."

"I am glad I was there when I was needed," the Duke said with an effort. "However, your Father has made it very clear what he expects."

Lynda looked puzzled.

"Expects?" she questioned.

"That I must now of course ask you to do me the honour of becoming my wife."

Lynda stared at him as if she could not believe what she had heard.

Then she said incredulously:

"Your . . . wife? Of course not! I have no desire to marry, you least of all . . . !"

She stopped, realising she was about to be extremely rude.

She could not imagine why the Duke of Buckington was speaking in such an extraordinary manner.

But the Duke also seemed surprised as he said:

"Your Father has not spoken to you about this?"

"Spoken—about what?" Lynda enquired. "I do not understand, Your Grace, what are you talking about."

"Then I had better make it clear," the Duke said in a sarcastic tone. "Your Father, and apparently most of the people staying here, think I have compromised you by saving you from a watery grave."

He sighed and then continued:

"In which case, Lady Lynda, I am obliged to make reparation for the sin I have committed by making you my wife."

There was no doubt from the tone of his voice what he felt about it. Lynda walked towards the door.

"All I can say, Your Grace," she replied, "is that if this is your idea of a joke, then I find it in very bad taste!"

She opened the door and walked out, leaving the Duke staring after her.

*   *   *

Having left the Music-Room, Lynda ran upstairs to her bedroom.

She told herself that the Duke of Buckington, whom she had always disliked, must have had too much to drink at dinner.

She did not for a moment take his proposal seriously.

She only thought he was even more obnoxious than she had expected him to be.

The Duke, on the other hand, went back to the Drawing-Room, where he found the Duke of Marlowe alone.

He looked at him enquiringly, and the Duke of Buckington said:

"You did not warn your daughter what was expected. She, therefore, thought I was playing on her a somewhat unpleasant joke. In fact, she replied that she had no intention of marrying anyone—least of all me!"

It took the Duke of Marlowe a few seconds to realise what had happened before he said heavily:

"My dear Buck, it was my fault for not having informed Lynda that you were about to propose marriage to her. She is young and innocent of the Social World, having just come from School. Leave everything to me. I assure you there will be no trouble in the future."

The Duke of Buckington did not reply.

He merely left the Drawing-Room, walked into the hall, and out through the front-door.

His horses were in the stables.

He went there feeling they would be more of a comfort to him at this moment than any human being.

He decided as he walked towards the stalls that he would leave the Castle early in the morning.

The Duke of Marlowe could deal with his own daughter!

He only hoped she would be adamant in her refusal to marry him; but it was too much to hope that he would be so lucky.

He was well aware of his own importance where the matrimonial stakes were concerned.

He knew too that the Duke of Marlowe would

not let him off the hook if it was humanly possible.

"Dammit!" he swore to himself as he patted his horses. "I have a good mind to go abroad and stay there! Why should I trouble myself with a girl who does not want me—and whom I have no wish to acquire as my wife?"

The Duke had shied away from the idea of being married ever since it had been first suggested to him by his Grandmother when he was twenty-one.

"The sooner you are married the better, as you have come into the title so early," she said. "You need a wife to help you, and prevent you from being pursued by all those glamorous creatures who swarm round you like bees at a honey-pot."

"I enjoy the company of what you call 'those glamorous creatures,' Grandmama," he replied politely. "I have no wish at the moment to saddle myself with the sort of wife of whom you would approve."

That had been the first of the endless remarks made by his relatives.

"You must settle down, Buck, and produce an heir," they repeated over and over again.

After two years, however, he had learned how to deal with the situation very effectively.

"There is plenty of time," he would say, "and when I do take a wife, she will doubtless surprise you!"

As it happened, he had every intention of

filling his Mother's place with someone who would be a credit to the family.

She would be the right sort of person to be the Mother of his children.

What he had never expected was that a situation like this would be forced upon him.

The unwritten laws of social behaviour, however, were very clear.

In these circumstances, he had to ask a tiresome girl he had never seen until to-day to become his Duchess.

Nevertheless he found it hard to credit that she had refused him.

He had never expected that any woman would say no to the prospect of being his wife.

She would be the Duchess of Buckington, hereditary Lady-of-the-Bedchamber to the Queen, and of importance in a hundred different ways which equalled his own.

He told himself that in a way he could understand that Lady Lynda had thought he was joking.

'I suppose I should have contrived to propose to her in a more romantic manner,' he thought.

Heavens above, he had enough experience with women to know what they wanted.

Love! Love! Love!

Did any woman ever speak of anything else?

Not as far as he was concerned.

He could not remember when he had been with a woman alone and they had not responded to him.

They invariably became even more ardent than he felt himself.

With a shrug of his shoulders he told himself that Marlowe must cope with the situation.

He could leave it to him.

He would return to London and the women who responded to him almost too eagerly the moment he looked at them.

Only later, when he got into bed without saying good-night to anyone, did the Duke ask bitterly why Fate should have paid him such a dirty trick.

It was then he remembered how Harry had cursed him a year ago when he had beaten him here at the Point-to-Point.

"He will be crowing over me now!" the Duke told himself.

It was then he wished, as a million men have wished before him, that he could put back the clock.

He would have then let a tiresome, unknown female drown.

chapter three

WHEN Lynda came down for breakfast the next morning, she was relieved to find that several of the house-party had left, including the Duke.

She, therefore, found herself having breakfast with the Countess of Eversham.

There was also a male guest present, but having finished his coffee, he left the room.

"You certainly caused a commotion yesterday!" the Countess remarked in a condescending voice.

"I had no wish to do so," Lynda replied. "I have always gone into the woods by that particular bridge and had no idea it was broken."

The Countess gave a supercilious smile, as if

she did not believe her.

Then she said:

"And of course it would be the Duke who passed by at precisely that moment. The way he rescued you will certainly be a story that everyone in London will relish."

Lynda knew that the Countess was deliberately provoking her, so she did not reply.

"As your dear Mother is no longer with us," the Countess went on, "I feel I should caution you to behave as she would expect. The last thing she would want would be for you to be involved with the Duke of Buckington, whose reputation leaves much to be desired!"

Lynda made no effort to finish her breakfast.

Instead, she said:

"I assure Your Ladyship I had no wish to fall into the water and nearly drown. While I am extremely grateful to His Grace, I see no reason why the episode should be talked about, or even remembered!"

As she finished speaking, she walked from the room.

As she shut the door behind her, however, she heard the Countess laugh.

Angrily she told herself that she hated them all.

If that was the sort of Society she was going to London to join, she had much better stay in the country.

She decided to go to the stables and look

at the horses; she remained there for about an hour.

She was hoping that, by the time she returned to the Castle, the rest of the guests would have left.

She was right.

When she walked back, the Butler told her that everybody had gone and that her Father was in his Study.

"His Grace wishes to see you, M'Lady," he added.

"And I want to speak to him," Lynda replied.

Because she was eager to be with her Father, she ran down the corridor and opened the door of the Study.

The Duke was seated at a fine Regency desk which had come into the family at the time of George IV.

It was very impressive with its gold mountings.

There was also a gold ink-pot which had been a present from the King when he had stayed at Marlowe Castle.

Lynda shut the door behind her and said ruefully:

"I hear they have all gone, Papa, and now I can talk to you."

The Duke held out his arms.

She ran to his desk and kissed him affectionately.

"I love you, Papa," she said, "and it is wonderful to be home."

"And I am very glad to have you back," the Duke replied.

He looked at her quizzically before he said:

"I think, my precious, you have something to tell me."

Lynda opened her eyes wide in surprise.

Then she said:

"Nothing in particular—oh! unless you mean the peculiar way in which the Duke of Buckington behaved yesterday evening."

"Of course I mean that," her Father answered, "and I can imagine nothing more important than your marriage."

Lynda gave a little gasp.

"My—marriage?" she repeated. "Surely, you are not suggesting, Papa, that I should accept the Duke's absurd and . . . ridiculous proposal?"

"Of course I am suggesting it!" the Duke replied. "It is the best thing that could possibly have happened. I was hoping you would make a good marriage, but I did not aspire so high as the Duke of Buckington!"

Lynda was so astonished that she could not speak.

Then, after a moment, she said:

"You cannot be serious, Papa! How could I possibly marry a man I saw for the first time yesterday, and who, as it happens, I detest and despise!"

"You do not know what you are talking about," her Father said so sharply that she looked at him in surprise. "Buckington is the most important Duke in the country. He is enormously rich, and his position at Court is unassailable."

"But you have all those things," Lynda said, "and I have no intention of marrying a man I do not love!"

The Duke leaned back in his chair.

"Now, let me make this quite clear," he said, "Buckington has proposed to you with my permission. I have accepted him as my future son-in-law and I am very glad indeed to have him in that position."

"I think, Papa," Lynda said, forcing herself to control her voice, "you are forgetting it is I who would be marrying him—and the answer is no!"

The Duke stared at his daughter, then his eyes darkened.

"Are you telling me," he said, "that you are refusing the greatest catch in the Kingdom, and a man who would be of immense benefit to me, apart from anything else?"

"*I* would be marrying him, Papa, not *you*!" Lynda retorted.

Her Father rose from the desk to walk across the room.

He stood in his habitual position with his back to the fireplace.

"Now, let me make this quite clear," he said firmly, "you will marry Buckington and thank God on your knees for the chance of being able to capture anyone so distinguished."

"I will not marry him!" Lynda argued. "I realise now that you have made him ask me only because of the unpleasant remarks made by the Countess of Eversham and some other members of your house-party."

She paused to say more violently:

"Very well! If that is going to prevent me from taking my place in London Society, I will stay here! I will be perfectly happy once the bridge has been mended so that I can reach the wood without being drowned!"

The Duke had gone red in the face.

He walked across the room and back again in an obvious effort not to shout at his daughter, as he felt inclined to do.

When once again he was standing in front of the fireplace, he said:

"I think you have forgotten, Lynda, that as you are not yet of age and I am your Father, you must obey me. You will marry the Duke of Buckington and there will be no more argument about it."

"I will not marry him, Papa!" Lynda said quietly. "And if Mama were alive, she would not make me."

It seemed a long time before the Duke said:

"Very well, then I had better tell you the truth. If you do not marry Buckington, I shall have to close up the Castle."

"Close up the Castle?" Lynda exclaimed in astonishment.

"It will be shut up and left to fall to the ground," the Duke said. "The old servants will have to go into the Workhouse, the horses sold, and everyone on the Estate will be dismissed."

"I do not know what you are talking about!" Lynda said. "What are you saying?"

"I am saying," the Duke replied, "that I am completely and absolutely broke. I am heavily in debt and I was banking on you, when we reached London, making a good marriage."

His voice seemed to break before he added:

"I never imagined that you would be fortunate enough to even be noticed by Buckington."

Lynda was still staring at him, her eyes very wide. The colour had left her face.

Then in a voice that quavered, she asked:

"Are you . . . telling me the . . . truth, Papa, and are things . . . really as bad as that?"

"They are worse!" the Duke said. "I was just banking on you, as I have already told you. I have been putting off my creditors with one excuse after another until you came back from France."

Lynda gave a deep sigh.

"I cannot . . . believe . . . it!" she said.

"I suppose I have been a fool," the Duke admitted in a low voice. "I should have taken steps before now to stop spending and perhaps to sell some of the things in the Castle which will make money in the Salerooms!"

He paused and then continued:

"But I kept hoping and believing that our

51

luck would change, and now, by what seems almost a miracle, it has!"

"How . . . can things be as . . . bad as you . . . make out?" Lynda exclaimed desperately.

"They were bad enough before your Mother died," the Duke answered, "but as you know, I loved her too much to let her worry over financial matters, and, as I say, I just hoped things would get better."

He walked across the room again as if he could not keep still before he said:

"We had a bad harvest and the farm-houses are in a terrible state of repair."

"But you . . . went on . . . entertaining," Lynda reminded him.

"I had only the Steeple-Chase and the Point-to-Point, which I have every year. It would have caused a great deal of comment if I had cancelled them, but for the first time I charged a fee to those who entered for the events. It gave me enough not only to cover the prize money, but also put a few guineas into my own pocket."

Lynda knew from the way her Father was speaking that he had felt humiliated at having to do such a thing.

Then, before she could say anything, the Duke went on:

"But that is just a 'drop in the ocean.' I owe money to the Butcher in the village, the man who supplies me with oats for the horses—his bill has not been paid for six months—and the same applies in London."

He made a gesture with his hands before he said:

"I have tried—God knows, I have tried to sell Marlowe House in Park Lane! But nobody wants a house of that size and the roof requires hundreds of pounds spent on it. Like the Castle, the ceilings are falling in because of the damp."

Lynda put her hands up to her face.

She was trying to think clearly, but she knew now that her Father was speaking the truth.

"I did not want to tell you this," the Duke went on, "but I have already sold most of your Mother's jewellery."

"Oh, no, Papa!" Lynda cried.

Ever since she could remember, she had loved the jewels that her Mother had worn.

She had thought as she was coming home from France how she would cherish them.

Also, if she wore some of the same things that her Mother had worn at Balls in London, she would feel that her Mother was still with her.

"I knew it would upset you," the Duke said, "but with the creditors knocking on the door every day, I had to give them something!"

"I . . . understand, Papa," Lynda murmured dully.

"I hope you *do* understand," the Duke said, "that the only way you can save me and your home is if you marry Buckington."

"But he has . . . no wish to . . . marry me," Lynda protested.

"He has to marry sooner or later," the Duke argued. "He will need an heir, and if you think he is looking for somebody he will love, then you are not facing reality."

"Why not?" Lynda asked aggressively.

"Because," the Duke answered, "men like Buckington 'sow their wild oats' and he has sown a good crop of them among the older women who are already married, as well as actresses and dancers, of whom you know nothing."

He glanced at his daughter to see if she was listening, and continued:

"But, when it comes to marriage, a man like Buckington chooses a woman whose blood is the equal of his own and whose lineage will embellish his family-tree."

"But you and . . . Mama loved . . . each other," Lynda objected in a low voice.

"We were exceptionally lucky," her Father said, "but I never thought, I never envisaged for a moment, that I would be fortunate enough to have someone I really loved as my wife."

"Is that true?" Lynda enquired. "But, surely, Papa, you did not behave in the same way that the Duke of Buckington has?"

Her father gave a rueful laugh.

"Of course I did! I also 'sowed my wild oats,' although not as wildly as Buckington because I could not afford it. But I enjoyed what you might call the 'Flesh Pots,' and was in no hurry to settle down until I met your Mother."

His voice softened, and it was very moving as he said:

"After that there was no other woman in the world except her."

"I do understand, Papa," Lynda said, "and that is what I want—someone who will marry me because I am me, and not because I am your daughter. And I want a man because he is a *man*, not because he is rich and a Duke."

The Duke of Marlowe put his hands on her shoulders.

"And that is what I want for you, my Dearest," he said, "but as it is, we cannot wait. Apart from that, if you searched the whole of London Society, you will not find anyone as rich as Buckington."

Lynda rose from the chair in which she was sitting to walk to the window.

It passed through the Duke's mind that that was exactly what Buckington had done.

He took out his handkerchief and wiped his eyes.

He was well aware that this conversation was of vital importance.

He was fighting for everything that mattered to him.

He loved the Castle.

It had been his home from the moment he was born, and he knew that to part with it would be like tearing his heart out.

There were also the horses, many of which he had bred himself.

If his daughter did not do as he wished, he could no longer afford to keep them, nor run them in the races at Ascot and Goodwood.

He understood, more or less, what Lynda was thinking.

He was aware that because of his love for his wife and hers for him, their only child had been born of love.

Lynda had been brought up in an atmosphere which was very different from that in the houses they visited and the people they knew.

Marriages were arranged amongst the Royalty.

In the same way, Aristocrats chose the Bride for their eldest son who would look right at the end of his table.

Lynda would behave in the manner expected of her, and a Duke, a Marquess, or an Earl could not ask for more than that.

If they had "interests" elsewhere after marriage, they did so discreetly.

Their wives, at any rate, would know nothing about it.

It was an unwritten law that, in public, they should behave towards each other with the utmost discretion.

In the majority of marriages, this was exactly what happened.

It was certainly what the Queen demanded from those in attendance upon her.

Waiting in silence while Lynda stood at the window, the Duke felt as if, like a drowning man, he saw his life passing before his eyes.

He saw the mistakes he had made; the opportunities he had missed.

At the same time, he knew that he and his wife were held in high respect by those who worked on the Estate, by those who lived in the villages and farms, and by the friends he had made at race-meetings.

It struck him that he would rather be dead than have to leave the Castle.

How could he dismiss the people who trusted him? And afterwards try to survive the criticism and derision of those he had once called his friends?

The Duke waited, and he felt as if the sun shining through the window were waiting with him.

The birds had stopped their singing and the bees no longer buzzed around the flowers.

At last Lynda turned round to face her Father.

"Very well, Papa," she said. "I will . . . marry the Duke of Buckington . . . if that will . . . save you."

The Duke felt a wave of relief sweep over him.

Impulsively he held out his arms, but Lynda walked towards the door.

She did not look back; she only went from the Study, shutting the door behind her.

*   *   *

It seemed to Lynda in the next few days as if nothing were real.

She felt as though she were living in a strange dream from which she could not awaken.

Her Father's delight at her decision was very obvious.

He told her that he was going at once to London to see the Duke of Buckington.

He would arrange for their engagement to be announced and for the marriage to take place as soon as possible.

"I have asked him to lend me some money," he said. "Of course, I cannot demand as much as I require until you are actually married."

"Is there . . . nothing we can . . . sell, Papa?" Lynda asked.

"Nothing that would give me the large sum I need," her Father answered, "and just at the moment no-one seems particularly interested in pictures or the sort of furniture which was designed to fit the Castle."

Lynda knew this was true.

It was her Great-Grandfather who had done up the Castle.

He had added a whole wing and employed the finest Architects, besides ordering from the greatest makers of furniture in the whole Kingdom.

She felt, as her Father did, that she could

58

not bear to sell the mahogany sideboard and Hepplewhite chairs in the Dining-Room.

There were the Chippendale book-cases and the magnificent gilded and carved furniture which had been designed by Adam for the Dining-Room.

She thought her Father was doubtless right when he said that few people were interested in buying furniture which was created for a different type of house than their own.

But it was very embarrassing to know that her Father was borrowing from her future husband.

She wondered what the Duke of Buckington would feel.

She thought, however, that considering how rich he was, it was what he would expect.

He was preparing to sacrifice himself by marrying the Duke of Marlowe's daughter.

The more she thought about him, the more she realised how furious he must be at being trapped.

'He must be wishing that he had left me to drown!' she thought.

Then she remembered how Alice had suffered and thought that, if he had to suffer too, it was only fair.

"I hate him! He is dissolute and immoral!" she told herself. "However, I have to save Papa."

When her Father had left for London, she ordered the bridge over the stream to be repaired.

She had it strengthened and made wider than it had been in the past.

The level of the water had fallen because there had been no further rain.

When she was able to go into the woods again, the stream had dropped by several feet.

It looked quiet and still, and not in the least dangerous.

Lynda stopped on the bridge to look down at the place where she had fallen in.

She could not help asking the still waters why they had precipitated her into a situation from which she could not extract herself.

'Perhaps if I had drowned it would have been better!' she thought.

Then she remembered that if she had died, her Father would have been in the same predicament as he was now, but without a chance of being able to save himself.

She looked back at the Castle.

How could they lose anything that meant so much in the lives of the Marlowes all down the centuries?

How could she bear to think of the servants who now worked at the Castle, and who had spoiled her ever since she was a child, becoming penniless?

The old servants at the Castle behaved as if it belonged to them.

"We're 'avin' a bit o' trouble wi' that there roof agin," they would say.

Or, she would hear the old Butler say to her Father:

"We're getting low in the cellars, Your Grace, and we won't have enough to go round if Your Grace has a party."

"They are part of the family," Lynda told herself.

The same applied to the Farmers, the woodcutters, the gardeners, and the game-keepers.

They talked as if the Estate belonged to them.

Just in the same way that it belonged to their Master—the Duke.

She did not like to imagine the consternation there would be if they were suddenly told to go elsewhere to work, or starve.

'I must save them! I have to save them!'

She felt as if the birds in the trees were saying the same thing.

So were the rabbits that moved among the undergrowth.

And the goblins who she believed lived underground.

She thought she could hear them hammering away if she put her ear to the trunk of a tree.

In the morning she went to the stables.

The horses mattered as much as the grooms who looked after them.

In the afternoon she went into the wood.

When her Father returned, she was waiting for him, not eagerly, but apprehensively.

She was afraid of what he had to tell her.

As he got out of the carriage she knew by the expression on his face that everything had gone well.

He kissed her affectionately and said:

"It is good to be back! Is everything all right?"

"Yes, Papa, and there is a new foal for you to see in the stables."

"That is good news!" the Duke exclaimed.

He handed his gloves and cane to one of the footmen.

The Butler helped him off with his coat.

"It's nice to have Your Grace home again!" he said respectfully.

"Tell them in the Kitchen that I am hungry," the Duke said, "and I want dinner as soon as I have changed."

Lynda knew that this had been anticipated.

Mrs. Wells had been at the Castle for over twenty years.

She would have all the Duke's favourite dishes for dinner.

It was only when there was a house-party that a Chef was employed to help her because she was getting on for seventy.

She resented the fact that she could not manage on her own.

It was Lynda's Mother who had insisted that the food in the Castle should excel anything that other great houses could supply.

"I thought what we had last week at Blenheim

Palace," Lynda had heard her Mother say to her Father after a visit there, "was almost inedible. You know, Darling, that we can do better than that!"

As she spoke to her husband he looked at her lovingly.

"No-one does anything as well as you do," he said, "and that also applies in the Kitchen."

They both laughed.

Lynda had been aware of the happiness in her Mother's eyes as she looked across the table.

'That is what I want to feel when I marry,' she thought.

It was what she thought now.

Her Father went straight upstairs to change.

She had no chance of speaking to him until after dinner, when the servants had left the room.

Then she said in a voice which she tried to make sound calm:

"What . . . happened, Papa?"

The Duke drank what was left of the brandy in his glass before he answered:

"I saw Buckington, and he agreed that the announcement of your engagement should be sent to the newspapers immediately. He then went to the Palace to inform the Queen. He intended to see some members of his family later in the day."

"And the . . . wedding?" Lynda asked in a small voice.

"Buckington wishes it to take place almost immediately, as he wants to be back from his honeymoon in time for the Derby."

"Immediately!" Lynda murmured. "What does he mean . . . by that?"

"He agreed with me that, as you had few friends in London," the Duke said, "and, as he saw no reason for entertaining his, you should be married here in a fortnight and go abroad for your honeymoon."

Lynda drew in her breath, and her Father went on:

"His excuse for the hurry will be that his Grandmother has been ill for years and may die at any moment, in which case the wedding would have to be postponed for at least six months."

Lynda was about to say that that would be a very good idea.

Then she remembered that her Father could not wait so long.

With the greatest difficulty she suppressed the words that trembled on her lips.

Instead, she managed to ask:

"And the loan . . . did the Duke . . . agree to make you . . . a loan, Papa?"

Her Father looked slightly embarrassed.

"He did—in fact, he was very generous. He also made some suggestions about joining up our racing stables and breeding horses together which would certainly be of great advantage to me."

"I am glad . . . for you, Papa," she said.

Because, to her consternation, she felt the tears pricking her eyes, she rose from the table.

"I will see that . . . everything is ready in . . . the Drawing-Room before you . . . join me," she stammered.

Then she hurried from the room.

The Duke looked after her, and there was an anxious expression in his eyes.

'The poor child will never cope with him,' he murmured. 'How the hell did I get myself into such a mess?'

*   *   *

The Dining-Room was very quiet.

The Duke picked up his glass of brandy.

Then, as if he knew that was of no help, he put it down on the table and left it.

As he went towards the door he walked like an old man.

chapter four

LYNDA spent the next two weeks going to the woods.

She rode in the morning, then spent the afternoon there.

It was the only place where she felt comforted and unafraid.

Her Father suggested that she should go to London to buy some clothes for her trousseau, but she refused.

It was her Aunt, Lady Hillebrough, who came to the rescue.

She said she would give Lynda her trousseau as a wedding present and would buy the gowns herself in London.

She was always very well dressed.

The Duke was certain that her taste would be impeccable and Lynda would not disgrace her Bridegroom.

It was fortunate that Lady Hillebrough also had a daughter who was one of the Beauties always invited to Marlborough House.

The gowns that were sent to the Castle were therefore exquisite.

Lynda, however, did not look at them.

She withdrew into herself and tried to forget that the future was terrifying.

At night she lay awake in the darkness of her room where she had slept ever since she had left the Nursery.

It was then, she wondered pathetically, what she could do.

"How can I marry this man, Mama?" she asked over and over again. "And how is it possible that Papa could have got into such a mess when you were not there to help him?"

There was no answer to either of these questions.

It was only by a tremendous effort at self-control that Lynda prevented herself from crying tempestuously.

She knew as she did so that she would have a headache in the morning and look terrible.

That would upset her Father.

She realised, because he was much more conciliatory towards her, that he was feeling ashamed of himself.

She hated the Duke of Buckington even more

because she was hurt and unhappy.

She felt as if everything were pressing in on her and she was being menaced on every side.

The Duke of Buckington was like a great ogre waiting at the end of the long passage to gobble her up.

She knew she was being melodramatic.

Only when she was by the deep pool in the woods did she feel as if the birds were singing to comfort her.

The bees were humming, and she need not be afraid.

The butterflies hovering over the kingcups were waiting to carry her into a land where there were no problems.

Certainly no reluctant Bridegroom, hating her as she hated him.

The days leading up to her wedding grew fewer and fewer.

At first it was just three days ahead, then two days, then—to-morrow!

If she had not felt so desperate, she would have been touched by the presents she received.

When it was known that she was going to be married, everyone was excited.

The Duke said over and over again that it would be a quiet wedding because the Bridegroom might at any moment be in deep mourning.

Nobody listened.

Lynda was being married in the old Norman Church in the village and they were determined to give her their good wishes.

Gifts arrived every day at the Castle.

There were little lavender bags made by the village seamstress, a special comb of honey sent up by an old man who kept bees, and a pair of slippers from the village cobbler.

It was very touching.

But Lynda felt she was somehow cheating them by accepting their good wishes when there was no chance of her being happy.

The Duke of Marlowe was busy running up and down to London to see his future son-in-law.

Lynda gathered that they were making arrangements about their plan to combine their racing stables and also the breeding of a mare which for years had been apparently a great interest of the Duke of Buckington.

"Our horses will surpass everyone's!" the Duke of Marlowe said with relish a hundred times.

Lynda managed to reply:

"I am sure they will, Papa," in exactly the right tone of voice.

The day before the wedding Lady Hillebrough arrived with more boxes filled with gowns.

There was also a collection of hats that were certainly very becoming.

The *lingerie* was so exquisite that Lynda was not surprised to learn that it had been made by the Nuns.

"It is fortunate," Lady Hillebrough said, "that

my daughter, Marigold, had just ordered a number of things from them. She has given you what is finished, and told them to complete another collection for her."

"That is very kind of Cousin Marigold," Lynda said, "and thank you. You have been very kind."

"The whole of London is talking about your wedding," Lady Hillebrough went on, "and I can tell you that a lot of beautiful ladies are biting their fingernails in anguish, and countless ambitious parents are piqued to the point where they find it difficult to speak of it kindly!"

She laughed as she spoke.

Lynda only turned away, thinking that, if they knew the truth, no-one would envy her.

"Now, cheer up!" Lady Hillebrough said in a brisk tone. "I am tired of you looking as if you have lost a half-a-crown and found sixpence! And no man wants a Bride looking like a wet sponge!"

Lynda managed to laugh at this.

She thought it was a good description of how she felt.

As the shadow of mourning hung over the wedding, the Duke of Marlowe issued no invitations to his London friends.

He asked only his neighbours in the country.

He knew they would feel insulted if they were left out.

"Buckington wants to leave early," he said to Lynda, "so you will not have to spend hours shaking hands with a whole crowd of people who usually attend weddings only to criticise."

Lynda did not ask where they were going.

She supposed it would be to Buckington House, which was about fifty miles away.

If that was where he intended to go, they would not arrive until it was dark.

What happened then was something she did not want to think about, and she quickly changed the subject.

She knew she would be on safe ground if she talked to her Father of his horses, and especially about new arrangements he was making.

He was bubbling over with excitement like a School-boy, explaining how their two stables would be combined.

He told her how he would take his own horses to the Buckington stables at Newmarket.

How, according to him, they would in future undoubtedly win every Classic race.

The day before her wedding, Lynda disappeared into the woods.

She refused to even open the boxes which arrived at the last minute from London.

She sat down on the grass by the pool and looked into its still waters.

She felt that a nymph might rise up at any moment to tell her what was happening in the darkness of it.

"Perhaps I will never be able to come here again," she murmured in despair.

Even as she thought of it, there was a flight of white doves overhead.

Silhouetted against the blue of the sky, they were what was left of the doves that her Mother had loved.

She had kept them in dove-cotes outside the Drawing-Room windows.

When Lynda had been abroad, there had been nobody to care for them and they had gone wild.

Now they were flying over her head.

Somehow they seemed to bring a message that was one of hope and happiness.

For a moment Lynda felt her heart leap towards them.

It was almost as if her Mother were telling her that things would not be as bad as she anticipated.

She would find what she sought in the end.

"What I seek, Mama," she said, "is Love, and that is something I shall never find."

The doves had vanished, but the beauty of them remained.

The sunshine coming through the leaves of the trees seemed to dazzle her eyes.

Just for a moment, the darkness faded and there was light.

She felt her whole being respond to it.

Then she told herself she was being over-optimistic.

Getting to her feet, she started to walk slowly back to the Castle.

*　*　*

When the morning dawned, Lynda had already
been awake for a long time, although she tried
to go on sleeping.

She did not want to face what lay ahead.

She was called early, and she knew it was
on her Father's instructions.

She had some difficulty in persuading him
not to invite any of the family to stay at the
Castle.

"I do not want them to come, and you know,
Papa, if they stay with us, they will keep
asking questions as to how I met the Duke,
and regretting that, as we are being married
in such a hurry, I cannot have a grand wedding
at St. George's, Hanover Square."

It took her a long time to make him see
sense.

Finally, he realised that the family would
undoubtedly be curious.

They would naturally ask a number of
questions he could not answer.

By the time Lynda joined him in the
Breakfast-Room, he had already finished.

"You are late!" he said reproachfully. "Now,
hurry! There is a great deal to do, and I hear
from Driver that you have not supervised the
flowers in the Church."

Driver was the Head Gardener, and Lynda
replied:

"I am sure Driver has done his best."

"Your Mother always arranged the flowers at Festivals," the Duke said testily. "Driver, as we both know, is good at growing vegetables, but he has never cared for flowers."

Her Father's voice was still reproachful as he went on:

"I did trust you to make the Church look attractive."

"I doubt if anybody will notice how the flowers are arranged," Lynda answered. "They will be too busy looking at the Duke, and working out in their minds how much money he has."

The Duke did not answer, but rose from the table:

"I suppose I shall have to go and see to it," he said, "and for goodness' sake, be on time! If there is one thing a man dislikes more than anything else, it is waiting for his Bride!"

With difficulty, Lynda prevented herself from replying that she was quite certain the Duke of Buckington would be delighted if she did not turn up at all.

She knew, however, stating it would only infuriate her Father.

The reason why he was in such a commotion over the wedding was that he was afraid something would prevent it from taking place at the last moment.

Lady Hillebrough had arrived just before luncheon.

Afterwards she came upstairs to help Lynda with her wedding gown.

Very lovely, it was of course white, and the bodice was embroidered with pearls and *diamanté*.

"It may seem extravagant for such a small wedding," her Aunt said, "but you can wear it again on the day you are presented at Buckingham Palace, and Marigold is certain it will outshine anyone else's on that occasion."

Lady Hillebrough also provided a diamond tiara for Lynda to wear.

"It is not nearly as grand as the Buckington diamonds," she said. "I remember how Buck's Mother always outshone all the other Peeresses at the Opening of Parliament."

She sighed and then continued:

"She also had ropes of pearls, and a magnificent collection of emeralds."

Lynda was trying not to listen.

Instead, she was forcing herself to keep calm and unemotional.

She thought of the woods and the stillness of the pool.

Lady Hillebrough chatted on.

She described the late Duchess of Buckington's jewels, and the occasion when everybody had envied her because she outshone even the beautiful Princess Alexandra.

At last she said:

"I hope I have thought of everything you will require on your honeymoon, my dear—

and that reminds me—I never asked your future husband where he was taking you. Do you know?"

"I have no idea," Lynda answered vaguely.

"Oh, then it will be a surprise," Lady Hillebrough said as she smiled. "Surprises can be both exciting and disappointing."

Lynda did not answer.

She was thinking of one thing she would be taking on her honeymoon.

She had packed it herself, and it was very important.

Having put the finishing touches to the veil and the tiara, Lady Hillebrough clasped a diamond necklace round Lynda's neck.

"You look very lovely, my dear," she said, "and now I must go. Your Father is waiting to escort you to the Church."

Only when she was out of hearing did Lynda remember that she had not said "thank you."

She went to the window to look out over the garden.

She loved the view from her window, which she had missed when she had been in France.

When she came back to the Castle after she was married, nothing would ever be the same.

"Oh, why, why did this have to happen to me?" she asked. "If I had gone riding instead of going to the woods, I would not have fallen into the water, not been saved by the Duke, and not have to be married to him!"

She wanted to run downstairs and escape to

the woods through the back door.

They could wait for her in Church, and when she did not turn up, the Duke of Buckington would go away.

Doubtless, he would feel very relieved.

Yet if she did so, Lynda knew that all the plans that he and her Father had made would fall through.

Then the Castle would have to be closed and his creditors would come down on him like ravening wolves.

She sighed deeply and turned from the window.

As she reached the top of the stairs, she could see her Father in the hall looking exasperated because she was keeping him waiting.

"Come along, come along!" he said as she reached him. "I cannot understand why women must always be late!"

"Only by two or three minutes, Papa!" Lynda protested.

"I want you on time, especially on an occasion such as this," her Father replied.

He helped her into the carriage that was waiting outside, and got in beside her.

The horses started off.

They went down the long drive with its ancient oak trees on either side of it.

The village Church was just at the end of the Park.

Before they arrived, Lynda could see there was a crowd of village children and their parents who could not squeeze inside the small Church.

As her Father helped her out of the carriage, the women moved forward to cry:

"Good luck, M'Lady" "May you have every happiness!"

Lynda smiled at them through her veil as her Father hurried her onto the porch.

As soon as they reached it, the Organist started to play.

Lynda could see that every pew was packed.

Those at the front were occupied by her relatives and her Father's friends.

Those belonging to the Bridegroom were presumably on the other side of the aisle.

Every other space in the Church was occupied by the villagers, the Estate workers, and anyone who could be spared from the Castle itself.

They were all people Lynda had known ever since she was a child.

Again she felt she was cheating them.

They were expecting her to make a happy marriage, and proud that she should be marrying a Duke.

They had no idea that the whole thing was a farce just because she had been stupid enough to fall into the stream.

On her Father's arm, she reached the top of the aisle in a few seconds.

The Duke of Buckington was already there, standing with his best man.

Lynda bent her head.

She had no wish to look at him.

The Wedding-Service was short; the choir sang the hymns and the psalms extremely badly, as they always did.

The Vicar was old and his wife was tone-deaf.

Lynda was suddenly aware that she was saying good-bye to her childhood.

When the Register had been signed, Lady Hillebrough drew back her veil from her face.

Then as the Organist started up the *Bridal March*, the Duke offered Lynda his arm.

She touched it as lightly as she could, but she was acutely conscious of him, also of the gold wedding-ring which now decorated her left hand.

"I am married!" she told herself. "I am no longer me! In the future I will bear his name. I am his wife!"

She thought, perhaps because he was feeling as she was, they walked too quickly down the aisle.

As they moved through the Church-yard, the villagers were crowding round them.

Now the children were throwing flower-petals over them.

There was an open carriage to carry the Bridal couple to the Castle.

The village lads ran beside it for most of the way.

It gave Lynda the opportunity of looking at them rather than at her husband seated beside her.

She thought, although she did not look at him, that he was bored.

"And," she told herself, "doubtless despising the children's efforts to make their marriage a joyous occasion."

When they reached the Castle, Lynda handed her bouquet to the Butler.

Then she led the way to the Ball-Room, where they were to receive their guests.

There was a table on which the three-tiered wedding-cake, which had been baked by Mrs. Bell, stood.

It was decorated on top with a bunch of lilies-of-the-valley, which had just come into bloom.

The flowers looked slightly incongruous.

Mrs. Bell had, however, insisted that she must have something to put on the top of the cake.

Lynda wondered if the Duke would notice it, but thought it would be beneath his condescension.

She could imagine her Father feeling embarrassed about the Ball-Room, which had not been used for years.

It was in urgent need of repair.

She only hoped that the mass of Spring flowers which decorated it would hide some of the deficiencies.

The Bride and Bridegroom had a flower grotto on which to stand, just inside the door.

Lynda doubted if the guests would notice

anything else except them.

This was inevitably true.

They did not know the true story behind the marriage.

The majority merely thought them the most handsome and attractive couple that had ever stepped out of a picture book.

The Duke was undoubtedly the most handsome man in London.

And it would have been impossible to imagine a more beautiful Bride than Lynda.

The women present could not take their eyes off her gown which had obviously come from London.

Lady Hillebrough's tiara glittered in the sunshine coming through the long windows.

It seemed as if more and more people kept arriving every moment.

After they had stood for nearly an hour, Lynda realised that a number of the Duke's friends as well as her Father's, who had not been invited, were there.

She was quite certain they had turned up more out of curiosity than because they wanted to give them their good wishes.

There were certainly far more people present than had been anticipated.

She was not surprised, therefore, when the champagne ran out.

Although her Father demanded more, the old Butler told him in an audible whisper that the cellar was empty.

It was then that the Duke of Buckington, drawing a gold watch from his pocket, said:

"I think it is time we left."

"I will go and change," Lynda said.

"I will be waiting outside for you in *exactly* ten minutes," the Duke said.

He accentuated the word *exactly*.

Lynda obediently hurried away from the Ball-Room, and up the stairs.

Lady Hillebrough had chosen a very attractive going-away costume.

It was of a deep blue silk, the colour of Lynda's eyes.

People were always surprised that her eyes were not the blue of the sky.

But, as somebody had once said, they were the blue of the Mediterranean Sea.

"Ye looks lovely, Your Grace!" the maids who were helping her dress told her, and her Aunt said the same.

"You made a very beautiful Bride, Lynda, and I am very, very proud of you."

"Thank you, Aunt Edith, for everything you have done for me," Lynda answered.

Her Aunt walked with her from the bedroom to the top of the stairs.

"Try to look happier, my dear," she said in a whisper, "and remember, if it is any consolation, every woman here is envying you."

Lynda went slowly down the stairs.

Her Father was waiting for her in the hall.

She saw that beyond him through the open door, the Duke was seated in a Chaise drawn by four horses.

She could not help feeling that if she had to go with him, that was the way she would like to travel.

Then her Father was kissing her, the guests were wishing her "Good luck!" and a number of people on the steps threw rice and flower-petals.

When she was safely in the Chaise, the Duke raised his hat politely and they were off.

The horses were obviously fresh and required a great deal of controlling.

They drove for several miles without saying anything.

Then the Duke, as if he thought it was something he should say, said:

"I hope you are comfortable?"

"Very, thank you," Lynda replied. "And I am admiring your horses. Are they a new acquisition?"

"I have had them for nearly a year," the Duke replied, "but they are still somewhat obstreperous, as I have not had the opportunity of driving them as often as I would have liked."

Lynda thought this meant that he was too busy in London with the beautiful women he pursued.

The horses were kept in the country.

As they drove on, the Duke said:

"I suppose you have never driven a Four-in-Hand?"

He spoke with a note of derision in his voice which annoyed her.

She therefore replied sharply:

"As a matter of fact, I have! My Father had an excellent team which I drove when I was sixteen, and the friends with whom I stayed in France allowed me to drive their prize chestnuts, which was very kind of them."

"I am surprised!" the Duke murmured.

Lynda hated him.

He was implying that he thought her too stupid and too inexperienced to be able to handle horses in the way he could.

They drove for about three hours before they stopped.

It was not, as Lynda had expected, at Buckington House, but a small, attractive Queen Anne house surrounded by a very beautiful garden.

They drove in through some gates, and Lynda asked after what had been a long silence:

"Are we staying here? To whom does it belong?"

"It belongs to me," the Duke replied, "and it is exactly half the distance from where we are going to go."

Lynda's eyes opened wide.

"Where are we going?" she asked.

"You shall see soon enough," the Duke replied.

There was no time for her to ask any more

questions, because as he spoke they drew up outside the front-door.

Two footmen hurriedly ran a red carpet down the steps, and there was an elderly Butler waiting in the open doorway.

Lynda was taken upstairs to where the Housekeeper, rustling in black silk and with the chatelaine at her waist, was waiting for her.

She curtsied and said:

"Welcome, Your Grace, and may I wish you and His Grace the sincere good wishes of all the staff."

"Thank you," Lynda said a little shyly.

It was the first time someone had ever curtsied to her.

She thought it was something she must grow accustomed to.

She was taken into a very attractive and impressive-looking bedroom with a huge Queen Anne canopied bed.

As she looked round her she realised that everything was in perfect taste.

The dressing-table, the chests, and the mirrors were all of the Queen Anne period.

A bath was brought in and set down in front of the fireplace for her to bathe before dinner.

The bath water was scented and there were two housemaids to unpack an evening-gown, help her to dress, and arrange her hair.

She thought as she went downstairs that her Father would appreciate the luxuries that money could buy far more than she did.

At the same time, she could not help being impressed that everything she saw was in the style of Queen Anne.

Even the pictures seemed to have been painted by the great artists of that period.

The Duke was waiting for her in what was indisputably a very attractive Drawing-Room.

Although she did not wish to think so, Lynda was well aware that he was extremely smartly dressed.

His evening-clothes fitted him without a wrinkle, making him look even more impressive than he had at the Church.

There was champagne to drink, and they made desultory conversation before they went into the Dining-Room.

The table was decorated with white orchids.

Lynda admitted no-one could possibly criticise the excellence of the dinner.

She thought she would feel too nervous and apprehensive to eat, but she was, in fact, very hungry.

She had been too depressed to eat any dinner last night and too agitated that morning to look at the breakfast dishes.

She therefore enjoyed course after course as it was served by the Butler and two footmen.

Because they could hardly sit in silence, Lynda asked the Duke about his horses.

He told her what he and her Father were planning and also how interested he was in breeding from his own mares.

They had already won a number of the Classic races.

Because Lynda had heard this conversation so many times between her Father and his friends, she made intelligent remarks.

She thought the Duke looked surprised that she should know so much about breeding.

He also raised his eyebrows when they discussed the horses owned by other members of the Jockey Club.

When the meal was finished, Lynda asked:

"Shall I leave you to your port?"

"I never drink port," the Duke answered, "and I think, as we are both tired and we have a long way to go to-morrow, the sooner we go to bed, the better!"

They had reached the hall as he spoke, and Lynda said:

"That is a very sensible idea."

She went up the stairs without looking back to see if he was following her, and went into her own bedroom.

The maid was waiting to help her undress, but Lynda said:

"Thank you, but I can manage quite well on my own, and I have several things to do before I settle down."

The maid looked surprised, but she walked towards the door.

"Good-night, Your Grace," she said, "an' I 'opes as you'll be very 'appy."

Lynda did not reply.

She went to the bag, which she had told the maids who had unpacked for her to leave alone, and opened it.

She took out something from inside.

Then she sat down in an arm-chair beside the fireplace.

* * *

The Duke was certainly tired.

He had been very late the previous night.

Despite his protests, his friends at White's Club had insisted upon giving a dinner-party for him.

It was impossible for him to refuse.

He had always thought the idea of a bachelor's last party was a lot of nonsense.

It was really only an excuse for a number of men to get very drunk.

He was particularly abstemious.

He disliked not feeling in complete control of his senses, and also of his body.

He never drank three days before he was riding in a race.

He was very tall, but he liked to ride lightly in the saddle.

It had been half-past-two in the morning before he had got to bed last night.

He had had to rise early to reach the Church at the time the marriage was arranged.

Now his Valet, Temkins, helped him undress,

and when the man had left him, he told himself that he had no particular wish to make love to his Bride.

He knew that was what she would expect, however.

There was no point in starting off the marriage on a sour note.

As there was no communicating door between their bedrooms, he walked along the corridor, and then he knocked on Lynda's door and opened it at the same time.

To his surprise, the room was fully lit instead, as he had expected, just two candles by the bed-side.

A quick glance showed him that the bed itself was empty.

It was then he saw that at the opposite side of the room Lynda was sitting in a high-backed arm-chair by the fireplace.

He shut the door behind him and walked towards her.

"Not in bed?" he asked.

"I want to speak to you," Lynda answered.

"I should have thought it was a little late for conversation," the Duke said dryly.

Even as he spoke he had reached her.

He then realised to his astonishment that she was holding a revolver in her hand.

For a moment he just stared at it.

Then she said:

"Will you sit down and hear what I have to say?"

The Duke hesitated, then obeyed.

He crossed his legs and sat back, apparently at his ease.

"What is all this about?" he asked.

"I thought it only right that I should make matters clear from the beginning," Lynda replied. "I agreed to marry you, as I think you realise, to save Papa from having to close the Castle and be unable to settle his debts."

She paused and then continued:

"As I told you before, I had no wish to marry you, and I know you had no wish to marry me."

"Nevertheless, we are married," the Duke answered, "and we must, therefore, make the best of it."

"That is what I intend to tell you," Lynda said. "I will be your wife in public and I will behave, I hope, in the manner you expect from the Duchess of Buckington, but that is all."

The Duke was astonished.

He was an overwhelming success with almost every woman he knew.

Naturally he expected a young girl with no experience to be impressed with him as a man.

There was silence for a moment.

Then the Duke said:

"I understand the reason for what you are saying. At the same time, I think it is impracticable."

"In my opinion, it is the only way for us to

live," Lynda said firmly, "and to make certain that you do not touch me, I must point out that I am a very good shot!"

Quite unexpectedly the Duke laughed.

"I do not believe this," he said, "and I can assure you, Lynda, that no-one in London would believe for a moment that I am being held up by a young woman with a revolver simply because she does not find me an attractive man!"

"There is no reason why your friends in London should know about it," Lynda answered, "but I warn you, if you do touch me, I shall make certain you do not do so again. Otherwise in public, I promise you, no-one will be able to criticise my behaviour as your wife."

"And I have no choice in this important matter which concerns us both?" the Duke asked.

"None at all," Lynda answered, "except, of course, that I expect you to behave towards me in a manner that does not give the gossips too much to talk about where we are both concerned."

She thought as she spoke that that was an impossibility.

Of course they would talk about the Duke.

When he returned to London to the women he found attractive, they would soon know his marriage was a failure.

They had known before what he was doing.

They would now doubtless feel sorry for his poor, neglected wife.

She had not spoken aloud, but she felt the Duke had an idea of what she was thinking.

"I do not mind being pitied," she said aloud, "so long as it does not upset Papa or make me feel a fool when we appear at public functions."

For the first time, the Duke looked angry.

"I can assure you, Lynda, that I will behave like a gentleman and accord you in public everything that you expect from a Duke of Buckington."

He rose to his feet.

"Now that that is arranged," he said, "I hope you will put away that dangerous weapon and sleep peacefully. You can be absolutely certain that you will not be disturbed."

He spoke the words mockingly as he walked towards the door.

As he reached it, he turned back.

"Good-night, Your Grace," he said, and left.

chapter five

LYNDA came down to breakfast to find that the Duke had already eaten and was outside in the stables.

She ate quickly, then learned that the Chaise had been brought round to the front-door.

This time it had a different team of horses from those they had used yesterday.

When they set off, the servant bowing them good-bye, she said in what she hoped was a light, conversational tone:

"You have not yet told me where we are going."

"I keep my yacht in a quiet cove about thirty miles from here," the Duke replied.

"Your . . . yacht?" Lynda exclaimed.

He did not say any more, and after a moment she said:

"I will be thrilled to be in a yacht! Papa has often spoken of how he enjoyed the sea and he took Mama and me to Gibraltar once, but I was only eight at the time."

"Then I hope you are a good sailor," the Duke said.

They drove on in silence.

They only talked—again about horses—when they stopped for luncheon at a Posting-Inn.

It was getting late in the afternoon when finally they arrived at what the Duke had correctly described as a "quiet harbour."

Lynda saw that it was used by Yachtsmen, because there were a number of vessels with their sails furled, bobbing in the water.

The yacht was far bigger than she had expected.

She knew without being told that it was the very latest design.

It certainly looked very sleek, and she felt excited as she went aboard to be greeted by the Captain.

Almost immediately, Lynda was taken below.

There she was shown into an attractive cabin decorated in pink.

It was like walking into an arbour of roses.

She knew it was not the Master Cabin, and she guessed, seeing how it had been decorated, it had been used by the beautiful, sophisticated women with whom the Duke was usually associated.

Her luggage was brought in by two stewards.

Then a wiry little man arrived and bowed to her respectfully.

"I'm Temkins, Y'Grace," he said, "an' I'll be lookin' after you on t'voyage."

Lynda held out her hand.

"I hope I will be no trouble," she said as she smiled.

"Depends on how critical Y'Grace is," Temkins replied. "Some is easy, some is difficult, and y'can guess which be which!"

Lynda laughed.

"I think we shall travel very comfortably in this big yacht," she said. "Has His Grace had it long?"

" 'Bout two year," Temkins replied, "and he loves it like it were his child!"

Lynda thought this was something different from thinking of him only as a race-horse owner.

While they were talking, Temkins was unpacking very skilfully for her.

She thought that if she had to spend her honeymoon with the Duke, it would certainly be better to be at sea.

One of his houses, however luxurious they might be, would be restricting.

As it was getting late, there was no time to change for dinner.

She merely washed her hands, tidied her

hair, and went up to the Saloon.

It was beautifully decorated.

When the food was brought, she thought it was every bit as good as the dinner they had eaten last night.

They said very little while the stewards were waiting on them in the Saloon.

As soon as the meal was finished, the Duke said he was going on the bridge to watch the yacht proceed out of harbour.

"We will anchor in some quiet cove a little before midnight," he said, "and I hope you will sleep peacefully."

"I am sure I shall," Lynda replied.

She went down to her cabin, undressed, and got into bed.

She was very tired, because of the long drive yesterday and because she had hardly slept at all the night before her wedding.

She fell asleep as soon as her head touched the pillow.

*   *   *

Lynda awoke and could not for the moment think where she was.

Then, when she felt heavy rocking beneath her, she remembered she was on the yacht.

She was setting off to an unknown destination, sharing it with a husband she had spoken to only a few times since they had first met.

There was no doubt they were in a very heavy sea.

She wondered if the Duke would expect her to appear in the Saloon for breakfast.

At that moment there was a knock on the door, and Temkins put his head round it.

"Be you awake, Y'Grace?" he asked.

"I have just woken up," Lynda replied, "and was wondering whether I should get up for breakfast."

"I'll bring it to you," Temkins said decisively.

He disappeared.

Lynda still felt a little tired.

It was a relief to know that nothing particular was demanded of her.

Then, as she looked at the clock beside her bed, she saw to her amazement that it was nearly eleven o'clock.

"Have I really slept as long as that?" she asked, and wondered if the clock was right.

Temkins came back, carrying her breakfast with extreme dexterity.

He placed it securely on a table built beside the bed.

"Now, Y'Grace had better eat wot I've brought ye," he said, "in case later you're feelin' sea-sick."

"At the moment, I just feel very hungry," Lynda said, smiling, "and I am horrified to find how late it is. I hope His Grace did not wait breakfast for me?"

Temkins grinned.

"His Grace be up on t'bridge like a School-boy at the start of his holidays," he said, "and if there's one thing His Grace enjoys, it's a really rough sea, which, if ye asks me, is somethin' we're about to have!"

It certainly got very much rougher as they proceeded down the English Channel.

Remembering the stories she had heard about the Bay of Biscay, Lynda felt a little apprehensive.

The yacht was soon pitching and rolling quite considerably.

To her relief, however, she did not feel in the least sea-sick.

Later in the afternoon she thought she would like something to read.

She was aware there was a small bookcase, built into a bulkhead in the cabin like the rest of the furniture.

She got out of bed and, looking at the books, thought they were what she might have expected to be in this cabin.

They were all novels, many of which she had seen the girls reading at School.

She decided none of them were particularly interesting and not what she wanted to read.

She waited until Temkins brought her her tea, then asked:

"Are there any other books aboard apart from these?"

"Books!" Temkins exclaimed. "If that's wot

Y'Grace wants, there's a whole cabinful of 'em opposite this one."

"A cabinful?" Lynda exclaimed. "Does His Grace enjoy reading?"

She thought perhaps it was a question she should not ask a servant.

At the same time, she had already learned that Temkins had been valetting the Duke ever since he had left Oxford.

" 'Course he reads!" Temkins said as if he thought she was stupid not to realise it. "And when we goes to a new place, he finds every book 'bout it, so he knows wot to expect afore he gets there."

He grinned before he added:

"Not that we don't get some surprises, one way or 'nother!"

"What do you mean by that?" Lynda enquired.

"I were thinkin' 'bout when we were in a Mon'stry in Tibet an'—"

"Tibet!" Lynda exclaimed.

Temkins's hand went to his mouth in consternation.

"There I goes agin," he said, "sayin' things as I've been told not to, and Y'Grace must jest forget an unfortunate slip o' the tongue."

"But why should it be a secret that His Grace has been to Tibet—if he really has been there?" Lynda asked.

As she spoke she found it hard to believe that

101

the Duke had been anywhere so extraordinary.

Then she realised that Temkins was looking at her in a somewhat strange way.

Finally he said:

"You'll have to wait for His Grace to tell you what he's been up to. If any man can clam up 'bout what he don't want people to know, it's the Duke o' Buckington!"

Lynda was incredulous.

At the same time, she thought that Temkins was talking nonsense.

Her Father had talked of nothing but him for the past fortnight.

Of all the things she had heard about the Duke of Buckington from one person to another, no-one had ever suggested that he was a traveller.

Because she was curious, she got out of bed.

Putting on a very attractive *negligée*, which had been made in London, cautiously she opened the door of her cabin.

She found, as she expected, there was nobody about.

She had not even heard the Duke all day.

She was sure that he would be on the bridge enjoying, as Temkins had said, the roughness of the sea.

She had to balance herself very carefully to cross the passage.

Then she opened the door of the cabin opposite.

What she saw when she entered filled her at first with astonishment, then with delight.

The cabin was obviously the Duke's private Sitting-Room.

There was a desk against one wall, a sofa, and two comfortable arm-chairs.

What delighted her was that three of the walls were lined entirely with bookshelves that reached from floor to ceiling.

Holding on to one of the shelves, she looked in astonishment at the books that were contained there.

They were not in the least what she had expected would interest the Duke of Buckington.

Some of the books were old, and some were new.

Their titles told her that most were history and guide books of the various countries of the world.

Others were famous classics.

She had always wanted to read them but they were not included in the School Library.

Nor, for that matter, in her Father's Library.

She reached above her head to where there was a book entitled *The Holy Mountain*.

Then a voice behind her said:

"I think you will find that one rather heavy going."

Lynda turned round, and almost lost her balance.

The Duke had come into the cabin.

Only the sound of the engines had prevented her from hearing him.

As she held on to the side of the sofa to prevent herself from falling, the Duke said:

"I think you had better sit down."

As he spoke, he did so himself in one of the chairs.

Lynda obeyed him, and thought as she looked at him that he was extremely smart.

He was wearing white trousers and a dark blue yachting jacket with gold-crested buttons.

She had no idea that the Duke was surprised to see her hair.

It was falling over her shoulders, almost to her waist.

Moreover, he had expected her to be prostrate in her cabin.

"I . . . I came to get . . . something to read," Lynda said.

She felt she must make some explanation.

"There are some of the latest novels in your cabin," the Duke said. "I told my Secretary to be certain they were sent aboard before we arrived."

"I saw them," Lynda said, "but I am more interested in what you have here."

The Duke smiled.

"But, as I have already said, I think you will find them rather heavy going."

"I was just going to take down the one on Tibet."

As she saw the frown on the Duke's face, she said:

"Oh, please, do not be angry with Temkins

for letting me know, quite by mistake, that you have been there. You are so lucky! It is somewhere I have always longed to visit."

"I doubt if you would enjoy it very much," the Duke said dryly. "The travelling is very hard and the Monasteries, on the whole, extremely uncomfortable."

"But you visited them," Lynda exclaimed. "Why?"

The Duke did not answer directly.

She knew he was trying to think of an explanation which would satisfy her, but would not be the true one.

"I had no idea you were a traveller," Lynda said quickly, "until I saw these books and learned that you must have been to many marvellous places, which I have only been able to read about."

"I thought young girls read only novels," the Duke remarked somewhat provocatively, "and that is why I am wondering what are your particular interests."

"Young girls grow older," Lynda retorted, "and become the beautiful, sophisticated women with whom you spend so much of your time."

The Duke looked at her in surprise.

She knew he was thinking it was a strange remark for her to have made.

Yet it was true.

At the same time, his conversation with older women consisted of really only one topic, and that was of course—love.

There was a twist to his lips as he thought of it.

"Exactly!" Lynda said. "But, while you admire them, as if they were flowers, you throw them away when they are faded!"

The Duke stared at her in absolute astonishment.

"You are reading my thoughts!" he said accusingly. "How in the world can you do that?"

The colour rose in Lynda's cheeks.

Because she was shy, she looked away from him.

"I . . . I suppose I . . . did it without . . . thinking," she said quickly.

"I do not believe that is the truth," the Duke answered, "and I will ask you again—how is it that you can read my thoughts?"

"If you really want to know," Lynda answered, "I will tell you."

"I do want to know!" the Duke said firmly.

"Well, when I was in School outside Paris," Lynda explained, "one of my Tutors was an extremely erudite Professor who had made a study of the human brain."

She glanced at the Duke to see if he was listening and went on:

"He had delved back through the centuries to when civilised man, who was little more than a monkey, had gradually developed a brain that gave him the intelligence of the Greeks, and the 'Third Eye' of the Pharaohs."

She thought as she spoke that the Duke would doubtless find this very uninteresting and said quickly:

"I am sure you will find what I am saying is boring."

"On the contrary," the Duke replied, "I am, as it happens, extremely interested, and if you do not believe me, you will find a book on the Pharaohs on the shelf over there which has a lot to say about the 'Third Eye.' "

"Then you will understand that it is what I try to do myself," Lynda said.

The Duke stared at her for a moment, and she said:

"I attempt to use my perception rather than to accept the judgement of others. Sometimes, therefore, I know what people are thinking, even though they do not express their thoughts in words."

"Now you are frightening me," the Duke said, "and I think I shall resent you knowing what is going on in my mind, whether I want you to, or not."

Lynda laughed.

"Then you will just have to think the right thoughts and be aware, as the Chinese are, of 'The World Behind the World,' which is the reason why they are always very polite."

The Duke laughed before he said;

"I find this conversation very strange and not in the least what I expected to have with you."

"And I had no idea," Lynda replied, "that your Library would hold the sort of books that I want to read, so I can only hope that this voyage will last for a very long time!"

She spoke what she was thinking.

Too late she remembered that this was an unwanted honeymoon with a man she disliked and who disliked her.

Then she realised that, if she could read the Duke's thoughts, he was reading hers at that particular moment.

His eyes were twinkling as he said:

"Perhaps we should both go back to 'Square One' and start again. I expected you to be a tiresome, stupid, rather gauche young woman interested only in her beautiful face. I admit now that I was entirely mistaken."

"Perhaps you are speaking too soon," Lynda suggested. "If you really have been to Tibet and other exotic places, you may find my ignorant questions, as I have been there only in my mind, very tiresome."

"That remains to be seen," the Duke said. "I have the uncomfortable feeling that I might not be able to answer all the questions you put, or tell you everything you want to know."

"I will be grateful for at least half, or even smaller mercies!" Lynda replied.

Then they were both laughing again.

The sea grew rougher towards evening, and Temkins refused to allow Lynda to leave her bed.

He brought her a delicious dinner.

Only then did she think she would rather be in the Saloon, talking to the Duke.

When she asked where he was, Temkins replied:

"His Grace be on the bridge, happy as a sand-boy, Y'Grace. Now, don't you go worrying 'bout him. Stay in bed and don't go breakin' any of your limbs tryin' to get about."

Lynda did as she was told.

At the same time, she could not help listening for the Duke to come down from the bridge and make his way to his cabin.

There was no chance to-night of them sheltering in some cove.

They just forged on through the Bay of Biscay.

At times it seemed as if the yacht were going to stand on its head.

When Lynda fell asleep she dreamt that she was swimming for the shore but could not find a place on which to land.

Strong waves kept sweeping her back into their clutches, and she would not survive.

She awoke with a cry to find it was morning.

The sun was streaming through the port-holes.

The sea was still rough.

Temkins informed her that the Duke insisted that she stay safely in her cabin.

Lynda wanted to defy him.

But with his order he had sent a collection

of books, which she had to acknowledge was exactly what she wanted.

There were two on Tibet which she found fascinating, one of which described very eloquently the customs of the country and the worship of the Dalai Lama.

When she had finished reading it, she felt as if she had actually taken part in the Services at the Monasteries.

"I wish he would take me there," she told herself.

She knew, however, it was an impossibility and something he would never contemplate for a moment.

The next day passed in the same way.

Lynda was beginning to regret that she had barred the Duke from her bedroom on the first night of their marriage.

She wanted to ask him to come to her cabin and talk to her.

Yet she could hardly send such a message via Temkins.

She knew after what she had said and done, threatening him with a revolver, that he would not come uninvited.

It was with a sense of relief that on the third day they had been at sea, she found the ship was moving much more steadily.

After breakfast Temkins told her it would be safe for her to get up.

"As I have not been sea-sick," she said, "I feel I am rather a fraud lying here in comfort while everybody else is moving about."

"I have no wish to have Y'Grace on me hands with a broken leg or arm," Temkins explained. "I've had enough with His Grace runnin' risks, coming back wounded when I were least expecting it."

"Getting wounded?" Lynda asked. "How could that happen?"

"There's plenty o' danger where he goes," Temkins said, "and Oi've told him often enough it's better to be safe than sorry, but he just won't listen."

Lynda paused for thought before she said:

"But why should he be in danger? And what for?"

Temkins looked at her in surprise before he replied:

"Seems His Grace ain't told ye 'bout his beloved 'Aladdin's Cave,' and it's not for me to chatter 'bout wot he wishes to keep a secret."

"His 'Aladdin's Cave'?" Lynda exclaimed in surprise.

"That's wot I calls it," Temkins answered, "but he don't show it to everyone, and I expects Y'Grace will have to wait your turn."

He went from the cabin without saying any more, and Lynda was intrigued.

What could the Duke be collecting—and why?

From all her Father had told her, the Duke's houses contained everything he could possibly want.

He had priceless furniture, pictures, and collections of all kinds.

They had been brought into the family down the years by each successive Duke.

"I must find out about this," Lynda told herself.

She had the feeling, however, if the Duke did not want to tell her something, nothing would make him confide in her.

Too late, she wished she had not been so aggressive on the first night of their marriage.

Because she had hated him, he had frightened her.

All she had been told by Alice had determined her to keep what she thought of as her "independence."

She was aware now, however, that he was very different from what she had expected. When she went up to the Saloon for dinner, she was excited.

The Duke arrived almost as soon as she had reached it.

"I thought you would get up to-day," he said. "It is very much calmer, and to-morrow we will be in the Mediterranean without a ripple to disturb us."

"I have been wanting to get up for the last twenty-four hours," Lynda replied, "but Temkins forbade it, and I felt I had to obey him."

"He is a remarkable little man," the Duke said. "I cannot think how I would manage without him. He takes everything in his stride and never makes a fuss if things go wrong. At the same time, he always speaks his mind."

Lynda laughed.

"I have found that out already!"

"I thought you would," the Duke remarked, "and I am sure you will be glad to hear that Temkins approves of your taste in Literature."

His eyes were twinkling as he went on:

"He says it is the first time any Lady I have brought aboard has ready anything except *The Woman's Journal!*"

"Of course there is no reason for them to read," Lynda replied, "when they can be talking to you."

She meant what she said sincerely.

She thought when she had said it, however, that it sounded somewhat cynical.

"While you, on the other hand, have managed quite well without me," the Duke said. "Now, tell me what you thought of the books I sent you about Tibet."

"They have made me long more than ever to go there," Lynda replied, "and perhaps one day I can persuade you into taking me with you, perhaps disguised as a man."

The Duke laughed.

"I doubt if you would make a very convincing one, and the Tibetans, with their acute perception, would be aware that you were a fraud."

"I thought of that," Lynda said. "But it seems

unfair that you should be able to go to such fascinating places while I have to sit at home!"

"Do you really think you would be amused by long treks on foot to unwieldy places, being threatened by tribesmen who take pot-shots at you for no apparent reason?"

"It all sounds fascinating!" Lynda answered. "But I cannot understand how you have managed to go to these places without the people who talk incessantly about you being aware of the fact."

"If I have deceived them, that is one feather in my cap!" the Duke answered. "And if you are really interested, I can tell you there are short intervals in the social calendar when it is easy to disappear."

He smiled before he went on:

"One of them is at the end of July, and no-one seems to wonder where you are in August or September."

He paused and then said:

"Again after Christmas, before the racing really gets under way, it is possible to go to Timbuktu and back again without anybody being aware of it."

Lynda laughed.

"I think it is very clever of you and I am only praying that you will be kind enough to take me, too."

"I will consider it," the Duke said in a lofty way.

She knew, however, that he was teasing her.

Luncheon was finished and Lynda said:

"I have been very remiss, I realise, in not asking you where we are going."

"To the Greek Islands," the Duke replied.

Lynda gave a cry of delight.

"The Greek Islands? How wonderful! It is where I have always wanted to go perhaps more than anywhere else!"

Then she asked in a different tone:

"But why? What are your reasons for going there?"

The Duke hesitated, and she knew that for the moment he was not going to tell her the truth.

Then, as he met her eyes, he said:

"If you are reading my thoughts again, it is unnecessary for me to answer that question."

Lynda drew in her breath.

"You have something special to find, something which you want very much."

The Duke did not answer, and she cried:

"Oh, please, tell me! It would be too unkind if you have all the excitement of finding a treasure and not share it with me!"

"I suppose Temkins has been talking to you again," the Duke said. "I cannot seem to make him keep his mouth shut!"

"He has told me nothing," Lynda said, "but I know there is something he calls your 'Aladdin's Cave.'"

The Duke sighed.

" 'No man is a hero to his Valet!' "

Lynda chuckled. Then she said:

" '*Many marvels there are, but none so marvellous as man!*' "

She had not intended to do so, but she quoted the immortal words of Socrates in Greek.

The Duke sat upright and said:

"You are not telling me that you speak Greek?"

"Both ancient and modern," Lynda replied, "amongst other languages. It was something I had to do in order to keep up with the Professor!"

"Are you speaking the truth?" the Duke asked incredulously.

Lynda laughed, and repeated the next lines of the poem in Greek:

> *Over the dark sea, he rides,*
> *In the teeth of the winter storm*
> *Driving through towering spray.*

"I suppose that is you," she said in English, "and you should be flattered that what Socrates said all those hundreds of years ago fits you so well."

"I suppose, if I were the right sort of hero to be worthy of what you have just said," the Duke remarked, "I should cap your poem with an equally true description of you! Unfortunately, and it is somewhat humiliating, I cannot think of one!"

Because it sounded so funny, they were both laughing.

chapter six

"WHERE are we going?" Lynda asked.

They had already passed several small islands like Paros and Naxos, and she wondered why they were still going East.

The Duke hesitated a moment, and she knew he was wondering what to reply.

At last he said:

"We are going to Cos."

Lynda looked surprised.

"But that Island belongs to Turkey," she said. "It is part of the Ottoman Empire."

"I see you are well read," the Duke observed. "As you doubtless know, it was originally Greek and almost the whole population is Greek."

"I did know that," Lynda answered.

They had sparred and duelled with each

other all the way down the Mediterranean.

Lynda made certain she could hold her own against the Duke because she knew it intrigued him.

"But why Cos?" she asked.

Again she had the feeling that he was keeping something from her, and she added slowly:

"I think you are looking for something, something that has been hidden, but you believe you will find it."

"You are using your 'Third Eye' again," the Duke said, "and it always makes me uneasy."

"But I am right, am I not?" Lynda enquired.

"You are right," he agreed, "and as you can undoubtedly read my thoughts, I might as well tell you that I am looking for something very precious which was found by a friend of mine almost four years ago."

"What is it?" Lynda enquired.

"The head of a statue of Aphrodite!" the Duke answered.

Lynda gave a cry of delight.

"And you really think you will find it?"

"I shall be very disappointed if I do not," the Duke answered.

"But, surely . . . ?" Lynda began doubtfully.

The Duke hesitated before he said:

"You are quite right. It is not going to be easy and we will have to be very, very careful."

"We?" Lynda enquired.

"You seem to be concerned with this," the

Duke said, "and, therefore, I suppose I had better tell you the story."

"It will be much easier than if I have to get it with my 'Third Eye,'" Lynda said.

The Duke laughed, before he began:

"A friend who is a famous Archaeologist went to Cos four years ago and he found in the centre of the Island a place which he is certain will eventually be excavated and will reveal a great Temple."

Lynda made a little murmur of excitement, and the Duke went on:

"He is certain that it will contain the statue of the great physician, Hippocrates."

"And it has not been excavated?" Lynda asked.

"No," he replied, "but my friend found a broken statue of Aphrodite and carried off the head."

"And you have seen it?" Lynda asked excitedly.

"Unfortunately no," the Duke replied, "but that is what I hope to do."

"Yet your friend left it there?"

"My friend was prevented from bringing it away, not by the Greeks, but by a riff-raff of young Turks who were determined that anything saleable on Cos should be theirs, and not left for the Greeks, who actually created them."

Lynda drew in her breath, but she did not interrupt, and the Duke continued:

"My friend had to run for his life back to the ship in which he was travelling to Cos. He, therefore, hid the head of Aphrodite at the foot of a plane-tree, of which there are a great many on the Island."

"What will we do if it is not there?" Lynda asked anxiously. "Have we far to go?"

"No. It is quite near the sea and my friend was furious at having to abandon it at the last moment. He thrust it down hard into the roots of the tree, knowing, because the Greeks think of them as sacred, it would be safe."

"And that is what we are going to find!"

"With any luck," the Duke agreed.

"Oh, Buck, how exciting," Lynda cried. "I shall be praying—praying very hard that we shall find it."

"I suppose, if I were sensible, I would not take you ashore with me," the Duke said slowly. "It may still be dangerous, and the Turks who were pursuing my friend may still be on the look-out."

"And when you find the head of Aphrodite—you intend to give it to him?"

"No," the Duke replied. "She is going into my 'Aladdin's Cave.' She will join a number of her contemporaries which I have brought back from the Aegean Islands and from Delphi."

"I cannot wait to see them!" Lynda exclaimed. "I am sure they will be wonderful, just as I imagine them to be."

She spoke in a rapt tone.

The Duke thought he had never heard a woman speak like that unless she was speaking of him.

He also thought she was looking very lovely in her simple muslin gown.

The sun was shining on her golden hair.

Every moment he had been with Lynda on the journey he had found himself being continually astonished.

First, at how much she had read and, secondly, how much she knew about the places he had visited, and especially about Greece.

Ever since she had learnt that they were going to Greece she had been in a state of excitement.

It reminded him of how he had felt when he discovered what he thought of as his first treasure.

They neared Cos just as the sun was setting over the ridge called "The Saw," from its jagged profile.

In ancient times it was called Prion, the Eastern part of the coast. Then, slowly they moved along a central lowland.

They reached the ancient Capital facing the mainland, where there was the fortress founded by the Knights of Rhodes.

Lynda longed to go ashore and see the Town itself.

The Duke, however, was determined to get as near as possible to where they were to find the head of Aphrodite.

The yacht pulled in close to the shore and had no difficulty in anchoring because the sea was calm.

They anchored near a place named after Xenophon, who was a descendant of Asclepius, the God of Healing.

The Emperor Claudius, who was always falling ill, engaged him.

He had a special veneration for the Doctor, who had been born on the island.

The great physician, however, repaid his Master a few years later by giving him poison.

When the Emperor vomited the poison, Xenophon pretended to help him by inserting a feather in his throat.

The feather was soaked in an even more virulent poison, and the Emperor died in agony.

When they talked about it, Lynda said:

"It just shows you how careful you have to be with Doctors! Papa always refused to let one examine him and he was very reluctant, when Mama was ill, to let the Doctors come near her."

"I am sure he is right," the Duke said. "Personally, I prefer to rely on Temkins and his 'honey and green fingers' where a wound is concerned. If I am laid up, he behaves exactly like my Nanny did when I was a child."

They both laughed, and Lynda said:

"I think Temkins is a wonderful little man!

He invariably has something amusing to say and when he helps me dress I am always laughing."

"I can say the same," the Duke agreed, "and actually, his skill with plants exceeds any other sort of medicine the Doctors can produce."

"We certainly do not want anyone poisoning us!" Lynda said.

It suddenly occurred to her that, if she were poisoned and died in Cos, the Duke might be delighted to be rid of her.

He could hurry back to London to the beautiful women with whom he had spent so much time in the past.

She was thinking of Lady Dalton.

Then she became aware that the Duke was watching her and was afraid he might be able to read her thoughts.

Because she could read his, she had a suspicion that he could read hers.

It made her feel shy.

The sun vanished and the stars began to come out like diamonds in the sky.

It was then that the Duke insisted that Lynda put on the darkest gown she owned and the most sensible shoes.

"I am sure we shall have to walk on a lot of rough ground," he said, "and there is the climb from the bay which my friend told me was up a steep path."

Lynda was excited by what they were about to do.

123

She changed in a few minutes, disguising herself further by putting a dark scarf over her fair hair.

When she joined the Duke she found he was wearing a black shirt and long, close-fitting black trousers.

The only touch of colour was a red leather belt round his waist.

"You look like a pirate!" she exclaimed.

"I hoped you would think I looked like Apollo, or one of the Gods," he answered.

"Apollo was the God of Light," Lynda reminded him.

The Duke was amused.

So many women had told him that he looked like Apollo that he had begun to believe it himself.

He was well aware that the Greeks never tired of describing the appearance of light.

To them, almost everything that shone was holy; the light was the giver of life.

If one were dying, it was best to die in the sun.

"That is what Homer thought," Lynda said, reading his thoughts. "It was he who said:

"Make the sky clear and grant us
to see with our eyes."

She spoke in Greek and the Duke said:

"Come along, let us spy on the Holy Land and hope that our eyes will not see light, but the head of Aphrodite."

As they walked across the deck, Lynda slipped her hand into his.

"This is very, very exciting!" she said.

Two seamen rowed them ashore from the yacht.

When they beached the boat in the sandy cove, the Duke lifted Lynda out.

"Wait here," he said to the seamen in a low voice, "and do not talk, as we do not wish to attract attention."

"We'll be silent, Y'Grace," one of the seamen answered.

The Duke walked ahead, and Lynda followed him up a rough path which led from the beach to the top of the cliff.

She could just see the way by the light of the moon, which was rising in the sky.

The stars were very bright, and when they reached the top there was no difficulty in seeing the flat field ahead of them.

It was a field where Lynda thought melons would be grown.

The Duke had told her that, with other summer fruits, they were exported from Cos to Egypt in small local sailing boats.

Everything was very quiet, except that in the distance she heard the bark of a dog.

There were a number of plane-trees, some small and newly planted.

The Duke walked determinedly in one direction, as if he were sure of the way.

Lynda was aware from the slight bulge in his pocket that he had brought a revolver with him.

She too had slipped hers into the pocket of her gown.

It was not heavy, but she felt it bump against her thigh as she moved.

She thought she might just as well have left it aboard.

They passed more plane-trees, then moved on to a very rugged piece of land.

It might have contained pillars that had once been part of a Temple.

Then Lynda could see the boughs of a much larger plane-tree which stood by itself.

She was certain this was the tree that the Duke was seeking, but did not ask the question.

She knew that he was afraid of their voices carrying in the darkness.

They reached the tree and he stood for a moment, looking up into its branches.

Then he bent down and started to dig with his hands at the roots.

It struck her that it would have been sensible to have brought a spade.

Yet there was, of course, always the chance that somebody would see it.

Then they would be aware that they were looking for loot.

The Duke's hands were very strong.

He dug deeper and deeper at the roots until,

at last, he located something hard.

Because the earth had been pressed down in the winter, it took him a little time to lift what looked like a huge round stone.

But when he had done so, Lynda, crouching down beside him, gave a stifled cry of excitement.

What he was taking from its hiding-place was undoubtedly the head of Aphrodite.

The Duke brushed the dirt away with his hands.

Now in the moonlight Lynda could see that the features of the sculpture were almost perfect.

The only damage was where the neck had been broken from the body of the statue.

"You have found it! You have found it!" she whispered.

"*We* have found it!" the Duke corrected her.

She knew he was as excited as she was.

He bent down to pick up Aphrodite's head, and the movement saved his life.

At that moment there was an explosive sound of a pistol being fired.

The bullet passed him harmlessly, hitting the trunk of the plane-tree.

There was another explosion, and a bullet hit the Duke in the shoulder.

It was then Lynda turned round and saw that two men were approaching them from the northern side of the field.

Without even hesitating, she drew the

revolver from her pocket and shot the first man through the heart.

She fired again, and hit the other man in the neck.

They both staggered and fell to the ground.

She turned quickly towards the Duke.

His left shoulder had been injured, and he was holding it with his hand.

"We must get away from here!" she said urgently. "Can you walk?"

"I am—all—right," the Duke replied a little unsteadily.

She could see the fingers of his hand were already covered with blood.

Putting her revolver back into her pocket, she picked up the head of Aphrodite.

"We must hurry!" she said, and started to walk back the way they had come.

The Duke followed her.

She realised that he was walking quite unsteadily.

At the same time, he was still clutching his shoulder and making no attempt to help her with her burden.

It was not far to the place where they had climbed up from the beach.

It seemed to Lynda, however, as if it took hours.

She was aware by the time they had gone only a little way that the Duke's steps were dragging.

She stopped for a moment to say:

"Put your left hand on my shoulder."

As if he did not feel well enough to argue, he did as she told him.

Despite the heavy weight, she managed to struggle on.

She was praying desperately that no-one would have heard the pistol-shots, and they would reach the path down to the beach.

She knew if that happened, other men would come to find out what was happening.

At last she was aware that they had reached the place where the boat was waiting.

Even as she saw the two seamen below her, the Duke suddenly sank slowly down onto the ground.

Lynda shouted, and the men ran up the path.

They picked up the Duke, and carried him carefully down to the beach.

Before she followed them, Lynda looked back, but could not see anything but trees.

She was sure that the two men she had shot were dead, or lying where they had fallen.

Then she was frightened.

Carrying the head of Aphrodite, she followed the two seamen and their burden down to the bay.

They got the Duke aboard with some difficulty because he was unconscious.

Temkins appeared, and helped them to carry him below.

Lynda watched them going down the

companionway and into his cabin.

Then she was aware that she was still holding the head of Aphrodite.

Temkins, having followed the two seamen into the Duke's cabin, turned back to say:

"I'll get His Grace t'bed, Y'Grace, then I'll come and tell you how he is."

"I cannot help?" Lynda asked.

"Not at t'moment, Y'Grace," Temkins replied.

She knew from the way the little man had spoken that she must leave everything in his hands.

She remembered how the Duke had said that he was better than any Doctor.

But she was suddenly afraid that perhaps the Duke would die from his wound.

Then her common sense told her that if it had been anything worse than a surface injury, he could not have walked so far.

She put the head of Aphrodite, which had caused them so much trouble, down in a corner of her cabin.

Then she started to undress.

She was too anxious to get into bed, and she sat in a chair, listening.

At the same time, she was longing to go to the Duke's cabin and see for herself what was happening.

It was about an hour later that Temkins came to her cabin.

"Is he . . . all right?" Lynda asked before the Valet could speak.

"He's sleepin', Y'Grace," Temkins replied.

"A-and . . . his wound?"

"Only a surface one," Temkins answered, "but Y'Grace'll understand that His Grace has lorst a lot o' blood, and he'll run a high temp'ture."

He smiled at Lynda as he added:

"His Grace be as strong as a ox! He'll be right as rain in a few days."

"I will help you nurse him," Lynda said firmly. "I nursed my Mother when she was ill, and I will do exactly what you tell me to do."

She thought Temkins might refuse to allow her near his Master.

To her surprise, he said:

"That'll be very helpful, Y'Grace!"

Lynda rose to her feet.

"I would now like to see His Grace," she said.

Temkins opened the door of the Master Cabin.

Lynda had not been into it before and she was impressed by its size because it filled the whole of the bow.

There was a very large bed in the centre of it.

As she neared the Duke's side, she saw that his eyes were closed.

His face was pale and he looked rather pathetic, more like a young boy than a grown man.

She could see that Temkins had bandaged

his wound very efficiently, and washed the blood from his hand.

She stood looking down at him. Then she said:

"If you will stay with His Grace to-night, Temkins, until three o'clock, I will take over then so that you can get some sleep. To-morrow night we will do it the other way round."

"That's very kind of Y'Grace," Temkins answered, "and y'understand—you mustn't allow His Grace to toss about, but give the wound a chance to heal."

Lynda nodded and Temkins said quietly:

"I thinks he'll sleep well enough t'night, but to-morrow and th' next day, we'll be havin' trouble."

"I am sure we can cope with it," Lynda replied.

She smiled at the little man, then went to her own cabin.

The horror of shooting the two Turks swept over her.

She was also exhausted from carrying Aphrodite's head, and having the Duke leaning on her shoulder.

When she got into bed she expected she would lie awake, worrying.

Instead, she slept peacefully.

She was dreaming of the woods at home when Temkins knocked on the door.

He did not wait for her reply, but opened it to say:

"It's three o'clock, Y'Grace. All's well, and His

Grace ain't stirred. Y'll find him no trouble, but if he moves, there's a bell by his bed that rings in m'cabin, and I'll come at once."

"Thank you, Temkins," Lynda said.

As soon as he had gone, she got out of bed, and put on her *negligée*.

She remembered how she had done this before when her Mother had been ill, so she took a blanket with her.

Temkins had arranged an arm-chair by the bed facing the Duke.

Lynda sat down, and put the blanket over her knees.

By the one dim light that Temkins had left she looked at her husband.

She thought that he still looked very young.

It struck her that there was no need for her to be frightened of him.

She realised that, ever since they had been aboard the yacht, she had not been so afraid as she had been at first.

Now, if she were honest, did she hate him?

How was it possible to hate any man who could talk to her about the Gods?

A man who was as familiar with them as she was.

A man, in fact, who looked like Apollo.

The body of Apollo that poured across the sky, intensely virile, flashing with a million points of light.

She had read somewhere that Apollo was not only the sun, he was the moon, the planets, the

Milky Way, and the stars.

He was the strange glimmer of the fields on the darkest night, and the glistening leaves in her woods at home.

'I want to talk to him just about things like that,' she thought. 'Oh, please . . . God, let him get . . . well . . . quickly.'

*　　*　　*

It was eight o'clock when Temkins came to relieve Lynda from her vigil.

"I hope you have had some sleep," she asked in a low voice as he came into the cabin.

"Four hours be all Oi' needs, Y'Grace," Temkins replied, "and Oi' hopes our patient has be'aved hisself."

"He has not moved," Lynda replied.

"Then if Y'Grace gets to your own bed," Temkins said, "Oi'll bring y'some breakfast."

It was just like being back in the Nursery, Lynda thought as she obeyed him.

Very shortly, Temkins appeared with a large tray on which was a delicious breakfast.

The sunshine was now pouring through the port-holes of her cabin.

She knew that the Duke, if he had been well, would have been up on deck.

Perhaps he would have been by now directing the yacht to some other Island.

Then she remembered the two dead men they had left behind.

Hurriedly she dressed and went up on deck to find the Captain.

"I think, Captain Bennett," she said, "that if the Duke were well, he would think it wise for us to leave here as quickly as possible."

"I was just thinking that was what we ought to do," Captain Bennett replied. "Temkins tells me His Grace is not too badly injured, but I know several shots were fired last night."

Lynda nodded.

"That is why we should get away."

"Is there anywhere particular that Your Grace would like to go?" Captain Bennett asked.

"I think Rhodes could be somewhere quiet, and the sea is smooth," Lynda replied.

The Captain smiled.

"I know exactly what Your Grace wants," he said.

"Then, please, take us there quickly," Lynda begged.

She had only just gone below to her cabin when she heard the engines start up.

It seemed incredible to her that she should have killed two men.

And yet, if she had not done so, she was quite certain they would have killed both the Duke and herself, especially if they realised what it was they had discovered at the foot of the plane-tree.

'We are very, very lucky to have escaped so lightly,' she thought.

She felt that her Mother had been watching over her.

If the Duke had not bent down, he would undoubtedly have received the first bullet in his head.

'Thank You, thank You, God!' Lynda said in her heart.

Later, she went up on deck to look at the Islands as they passed them.

Before they anchored she saw a glimpse of the coast of Turkey.

It was what she had read about, what she had dreamt of, but never expected to see for herself, except in books.

Yet now, the man she had hated had brought her to the land which to her was Paradise itself.

How could she be anything but grateful to him?

"He is different, so very different from what I expected," she said.

She wondered for the first time if he was more satisfied with her than he had been when he learned that he had to marry her.

Suddenly she felt ashamed of the way she had behaved on her wedding-night.

She knew now that her dramatic words and actions had been unnecessary.

She realised that if she had spoken quietly to the Duke without brandishing a revolver at him, he would have understood.

Just as now he understood what she was thinking.

"It was very foolish of me," she said, "and it would have been better still if I had talked to him *before* the wedding and explained how necessary it was for me to save Papa."

Because thinking of the Duke made it seem imperative to see him, she went to his cabin.

Temkins was not there.

The curtains were half-drawn over the portholes.

It was very quiet, and the Duke did not seem to have moved since she had left him at four o'clock in the morning.

His eyes were still closed and the skin beneath his sun-tan seemed very pale.

Lynda stood looking at him for a long time.

Then she knew that for her, at any rate, definitely and unquestionably, he was Apollo, the God of Light.

Very softly, so that it was just a whisper, she said in Greek:

*"Make the sky clear and grant me
to see it with my eyes."*

chapter seven

LYNDA was asleep when Temkins came with
her breakfast.

She knew then that it must be half-past
ten.

He always allowed her to sleep late when
she had been looking after the Duke at night.

She sat up, asking eagerly:

"How is His Grace this morning?"

" 'E woke up for a while," Temkins replied,
"it were after Y'Grace left, but he settled down
again, and now he's sleepin' peaceful-like."

Lynda gave a little sigh.

It was two days since the Duke had been
unconscious owing to a high temperature, but
it seemed more.

She wanted him to wake up so that she could talk to him.

"Now, don't you worry," Temkins said as if she had spoken aloud. "I've bin with 'Is Grace long enough to know he's always like this after he's bin hit. I remembers wot a state he were in after a poisoned arrow hit him."

"A poisoned arrow?" Lynda exclaimed.

"In Africa, it were," Temkins said. "When an unpleasant lot o' tribesmen were a-trying to get rid o' us."

He laughed as he started to tidy the cabin.

Then Temkins went on:

"Don't y'worry, Y'Grace. He'll be up on his feet afore y' can say 'Jack Robinson.' I only hopes he's not in a hurry to get back t' London."

"Do you think that is what he will want to do?" Lynda asked.

"Not with all them women worryin' him." Temkins answered. "They're a real nuisance—that's what they are!"

Lynda was still for a moment before she said in a small voice:

"B-but . . . His Grace . . . likes them."

"He wouldn't be human if he didn't think it a compliment they runs after him, but they goes too far! Like that lady—what was her name?—Dawes—no—Dalton—that's who her was."

Lynda was still.

Then she asked:

"Lady Dalton? Did His Grace find her a nuisance?"

"That be puttin' it mildly," Temkins replied as he put Lynda's *negligée* neatly on a chair. "Like a ravenin' wolf. Her never left him be for a minute! Trying t'bribe me so's she could see him when he didn't want t'see 'er."

Lynda drew in her breath.

"He really . . . did not want . . . to see her?" she murmured.

Temkins laughed.

"If I was t'tell you the things His Grace said 'bout her, ye'd be shocked! In t'end, he had t'go abroad for a month or two, jest t'get away from her!"

Lynda did not say any more.

She only thought how stupid she had been to hate the Duke because of what Alice had told her.

"There be good women an' bad women," Temkins was saying as he walked towards the cabin door, "and I always thinks that woman were bad through and through, besides bein' a nuisance!"

The way he spoke was so funny that Lynda could not help giving a little chuckle.

Then she told herself she had been very stupid.

She had judged the Duke without really considering that he might have a different point of view.

Of course, as Temkins had said, any man

would be flattered when beautiful women fawned on him.

At the same time, she could almost hear him say "Enough is enough!"

"When he wakes up," she told herself, "I will try and explain to him how foolish I have been."

She had a feeling it was not going to be easy.

* * *

The Duke was suddenly aware that he was awake.

Two people were talking in low voices.

"His Grace has been a bit res'less," he heard Temkins say, "but I've left the ice in a bowl. I don't think as Y'Grace'll need it. His temp'tures almost down t'normal."

"Is it really?" Lynda exclaimed. "Oh, Temkins, that is wonderful!"

"I thought Y'Grace would think so, and as I told y', he'll soon be on 'is feet again."

"Thank you, Temkins," Lynda said. "Now go to bed, and sleep well, and if it is after three o'clock, do not worry. I can doze quite comfortably here if he is not restless."

"I'll be with Y'Grace at three o'clock," Temkins said. "I sets me 'ead like an alarm clock, which I've learnt to do over th' years, an' a noisy sound it makes!"

The Duke heard Lynda give a little laugh as the cabin door shut.

He knew she was approaching the bed.

She came close to him, and he felt her hand on his forehead.

She touched him very gently. Then she said:

"You are better! You are much better, and now I want you to hurry and get well. There are so many things to see and do, and all Greece is waiting for you!"

The way she spoke, in a soft, almost caressing voice, made the Duke aware that he had heard somebody talking to him all the time his body had seemed to be in a burning fire.

To his surprise, he felt Lynda move onto the bed beside him.

Once again her hand was on his forehead, and he realised she was stroking it very gently.

"I looked at the Island to-day," she said, "and I am sure there is a Temple somewhere on it, but I am waiting for you to take me to see what we can find."

She paused before she added:

"We are a long way now from those nasty Turks who would have killed you. How could you have been so foolish as to think they were not watching to stop anyone taking the relics that they knew were hidden somewhere?"

She moved her fingers slowly up and down his forehead before she went on:

"We are free of them now, and it is the Gods of Greece who will help you, especially Apollo, whom you resemble. He was not only the God of Light, but also the God of Healing. He healed everything he touched, 'defying the powers of darkness.'"

Her fingers moved a little more positively as she continued:

"He was a painter who splashed colour on the sky and mysteriously turned the orange rocks to purple in the evening. He was the personification of light, and that is what you must be to the people who look up to you and admire you."

She gave a little sigh, then became even more positive:

"When you go back to England you must make them realise how much you can do for them. Those who admire you because you are a sportsman, and because your horses are superior to anyone else's will listen. You will inspire young men to follow you and to be like you."

Her voice deepened as she said softly:

"To the Greeks, light is their protection against the evil of the dark and that is what you must be to all the people who believe in you."

She took her hand away from the Duke's forehead.

Then, just as he thought she was going away, he felt something very soft and gentle against his cheek.

It was there just for the passing of a second.

Then once again the soothing fingers were massaging his forehead.

Without meaning to, he fell asleep.

* * *

The following morning, when Temkins appeared with her breakfast, Lynda was waiting for him eagerly.

She was already sitting up in bed, wearing a dressing-jacket.

The curtains were drawn back from the portholes.

As Temkins came into the cabin, she said quickly:

"What has happened? I heard you talking to His Grace! I know I heard you talking!"

"That's right, Y'Grace," Temkins said, putting down the breakfast-tray. "His Grace woke up at six o'clock and his temp'ture's normal. Now he's talkin' 'bout getting' up!"

"But . . . you will not let him?" Lynda asked. "Not until the wound has healed?"

"I tells His Grace," Temkins said with a note of satisfaction in his voice, "it's me herbs and honey that's healed him. There's only a mark now to show where them devils shoots at him an' they'll be gone afore long."

"Oh, Temkins, you are clever!" Lynda exclaimed. "I was so frightened in case it handicapped him."

Temkins laughed.

"It'd take more 'n that t'andicap His Grace. I'm havin' trouble, I c'n tell y', keepin' him in bed. I've told him:

" 'If y' don't keep quiet fer another twenty-four hours, y'll be puttin' yerself back a week, and that won't be to y' likin'!' "

"I am sure you are right," Lynda agreed. "My Mother always said it was a mistake, when you have had a temperature, to get up too soon."

"You leave His Grace t'me," Temkins said. "I'll make him see sense!"

He went from the cabin, and Lynda wished she could go with him and see the Duke.

But she knew that now that he was awake she would have to wait for an invitation before she went to his cabin.

It was something she waited for all day, but which never came.

Temkins, however, kept her informed of what was happening.

"His Grace has eaten some food, but now he's gone t' sleep again," he said. "As I told him—anyone as has lost a lot o' blood it takes time afore th' body works as quick as what it used to, but he's given me his orders."

"What orders?" Lynda asked quickly.

"He sends for the Cap'ain an' told him he's to move from here an' he's told him where we're agoin'."

"What have you found out?" Lynda asked quickly. But Temkins had already turned to go and didn't hear her question.

She had an idea the Duke had ordered the Captain to return to England.

Perhaps he thought the honeymoon had gone on long enough and he should return to his own friends.

'I must see more of Greece while I am here— I must!' she thought.

She wondered if she should get up now that the Duke was so much better and ask the seamen to row her ashore.

She had the feeling, however, that if she explored without the Duke, it would somehow be taking an unfair advantage.

"I must wait for him," she told herself.

At the same time, she was desperately afraid when the engines started up.

They might be on their way back through the Mediterranean, to the Bay of Biscay, and to England.

"Oh, please, please," she prayed to the Gods of Olympus, "let me stay a little longer! Let me see something of your land now that I am here!"

She wondered if they could understand how much it meant to her.

Instead of going ashore, she went to the Duke's Private Cabin and took out some of his books on Greece.

She found one which told her what she knew already.

During the miraculous fifty years when Athens became the centre of civilisation, Apollo and Athene were the guardians of Greece.

They were the youngest and sweetest Gods

who ever ruled, lovers of life and of the mind's free-soaring flight.

'That is something which no-one can prevent me from doing,' Lynda thought. 'At the same time, I want to share it with Buck, as Athene shared it with Apollo.'

It was then she realised that she loved the Duke.

She had loved him for a long time, but she had been afraid to face the truth of it.

Now they might be moving towards England, and it was too late.

Her whole being cried out that they must stay in Greece and discover how much it could mean to them both.

It was an agony all the afternoon to know that the Duke was so near her, and yet so far.

She heard Temkins leave his cabin and knew that he must be asleep.

She wanted more than she had ever wanted anything in her whole life to go in and just look at him.

Then she told herself that, if he woke and found her there, he might be annoyed.

She wondered what he would think if he had any idea that she had lain beside him all night and talked to him.

Her Mother had always told her that when anyone was unconscious, it helped them to recover.

"Talk to them," she had said, "and try to reach their heart rather than their brain."

It was what she tried to do.

'Oh, please, make him want to see me,' she prayed in her heart.

She thought because they were so near that he must hear her.

After she had dined alone in the Saloon she went back to her cabin.

It was then that Temkins knocked on the door.

"His Grace be fast asleep, Y'Grace," he said, "so if y're agreeable, Oi'll pop off for a bit of shut-eye 'til three o'clock."

Lynda felt her heart leap.

"Of course, I will look after His Grace," she said, "and you must have some sleep."

Temkins grinned at her.

"I'm all right," he said, "and so's His Grace—tough as leather, he be—after any accident."

"I hope you are right," Lynda said. "Goodnight, Temkins, and sleep well!"

"No doubt 'bout that, Y'Grace," Temkins replied.

Lynda heard him hurrying down the passageway.

She was already wearing her pretty blue *negligée*, as she had not got into bed.

She looked in the mirror to see that her hair was tidy.

Then she laughed to herself for worrying when the Duke was fast asleep and would not see her.

She was aware that the anchor had gone

down and they had stopped for the night.

There would be nothing to disturb him.

Not that during the past days there had been any danger of that.

At the same time, if they were on their way to the Bay of Biscay, it would disturb him if the sea was rough.

'I only hope he is not in a hurry to get to wherever it is we are going,' she thought.

She wondered what the Duke would say if she begged him on her knees to stay a little longer in Greece.

She had the frightening feeling that if he wanted to go, he would go, and nothing she could do or say would prevent him from having his own way.

She opened the door of his cabin very quietly.

Temkins had left the usual light burning beside the bed.

She thought, however, it must have been on the Duke's instructions that to-night the curtains were drawn back.

She could see the stars, and there was a new moon moving slowly up the sky.

She went to the bed and stood looking at the Duke.

His eyes were closed, as they had been every night.

But there was no longer the pallor which had frightened her.

At the same time, he looked even more handsome than he had last night.

She bent forward to look at him a little closer, and as she did so his eyes opened.

"You . . . you are . . . awake!"

She could hardly breathe the words.

"Yes, Lynda, I am awake," the Duke answered, "and I am feeling very much better, thanks to you and Temkin."

"You must really thank Temkin," Lynda said. "His healing herbs have worked wonders on your wound."

"But I also have to thank you," the Duke said.

There was silence.

Even as Lynda was wondering whether he wanted her to go away now that he was awake, he said:

"I want to talk to you, and because it is very important, I suggest you lie on the bed, as you have on other nights."

Lynda's eyes widened.

"H-how did you . . . know that?"

"It is true, is it not?" the Duke asked. "And as we might as well be comfortable, I suggest you take off your dressing-gown and get into bed. As you have already found, it is quite big enough for both of us!"

Lynda gave a little gasp.

Because he had spoken in such a serious tone, she suddenly had a terrifying feeling.

Perhaps he was going to tell her that he had thought of a way for their marriage to be at an end.

Then they could both be free.

Perhaps he wanted her to live abroad.

Perhaps he had some clever idea of dissolving the marriage which for the moment she could not begin to imagine.

He shut his eyes again, as if he waited for her to obey him.

Then because it was easier to do what he wanted than argue, she took off her *negligée*.

She slipped into bed, keeping as far away from the Duke as possible.

It was such a big bed that there was no contact between them.

For a moment the Duke did not speak, and she wondered if he had gone to sleep.

Then he said:

"I understand you have been here every night with me. That must have been extremely tiresome for you."

"Temkins had to sleep sometime," Lynda said quickly, "and I wanted to help you to get well."

"Why?" the Duke asked.

Because she was so surprised at the question, Lynda could not for the moment think of an answer.

"You hated having to marry me," the Duke said when she did not speak, "and if you had not stopped the Turks from killing me, as they tried to do, you would have been free of me."

He paused and then said:

"Of course, as a beautiful and wealthy

Duchess, the world would have been at your feet!"

"How can . . . you imagine . . . for a moment that I wanted you . . . to die?" Lynda asked angrily. "It is a . . . wicked thing to say . . . and of course I . . . want you to . . . live!"

"So you killed two men to make sure of it!" the Duke said softly.

"I am trying . . . not to think . . . of that," Lynda answered, "but you . . . know if I had . . . not killed them, they would . . . have killed . . . us."

"Me, at any rate," the Duke said, "and I am very grateful, Lynda, for being alive."

"We must . . . just forget about . . . it," Lynda said, "and when . . . you see the . . . head of Aphrodite . . . you will . . . know it was . . . worth the . . . risk!"

He did not speak, and she went on:

"I have cleaned her and she is very lovely, so I know how . . . proud you will be to put . . . her in your 'Aladdin's Cave.' "

"If anyone should put it there with great ceremony," the Duke said, "it should be you. You not only saved my life, Lynda, but you managed to bring away Aphrodite, and support me until we reached the boatmen!"

He smiled before he added:

"In fact, you are a very remarkable young woman! And very different from what I expected you would be like."

"And you are . . . different . . . too," Lynda murmured.

"Are you quite sure?" the Duke asked.

"Quite . . . quite . . . sure," she answered, "and I am . . . sorry for . . . all the . . . nasty things I . . . thought . . . about you."

The words came out a little hesitatingly.

The Duke suddenly turned round and raised himself on his elbow so that he could look down at her.

"What do you think of me now?" he asked.

Because he was looking at her and was so near, Lynda suddenly felt shy and could not look at him.

The colour rose in her cheeks.

The Duke did not move for a long moment. Then he said:

"Last night, Lynda, you kissed me, and it is only fair now that I should kiss you."

Before she could really understand what he had said, his lips were on hers.

For a second she could not believe it was actually happening.

Then a shaft of fire seemed to burn through her breast and she felt an ecstasy she had not known existed.

The Duke's kiss became more passionate, more possessive, more demanding.

She felt as if he were taking her heart from her body and making it his.

As he kissed her, the cabin seemed to whirl round them.

Then she knew that she was flying in the sky.

They were among the stars and the moon.

The light of Apollo was shining through them.

At last, as if with an effort, the Duke raised his head.

"Now, tell me what you think about me," he asked, and his voice was very deep.

"I love you . . . I . . . love you!" Lynda whispered.

"As I love you," the Duke said quietly, "as I have for a long time, but I thought you still hated me!"

"It was very . . . stupid of me . . . very wrong," Lynda said, "but I did not . . . know what you were . . . really like . . . and now . . ."

" . . . now you love me!" the Duke finished for her. "I adore you. I want you more than I have ever wanted anything in my whole life!"

"Can this . . . really . . . be . . . true?" Lynda asked.

"Do you think I would lie to you," the Duke asked, "when we are a part of Greece and it means more to us both than anywhere else in the world?"

"That is . . . what I feel," Lynda said, "but I was . . . terribly afraid that . . . when the yacht started . . . to move to-day . . . we were . . . going h-home."

"We are going to Delphi," the Duke said, "so I can show you where we both belong. I will also tell the Gods what I feel about you and you shall tell them what you feel about me."

"I love you . . . and I worship you . . . as Apollo!"

The words were hardly above a whisper, but the Duke heard them.

Then he was kissing her, wildly, fiercely, passionately.

She knew that no-one could feel such rapture and still be alive.

Only when he raised his head again did she say:

"You . . . must be . . . careful! I am . . . sure you are . . . doing too . . . much too . . . quickly."

The Duke gave a little laugh.

"Are you still looking after me and protecting me?" he asked. "My precious, it is something you will have to do for the rest of our lives."

"Do you . . . really and . . . truly want me?" Lynda asked.

"I want you with me every minute of every day and every year so long as we both shall live," the Duke said, "and what is more, my beautiful little Aphrodite, I shall be a very jealous husband."

He paused and then said:

"I want your thoughts to be of me, and that clever little brain which astonishes me must be mine, just as I want your heart and your exquisite and perfect body."

As he spoke, Lynda felt his hand moving over her skin.

The starlight was streaking through her.

Now it was more intense and seemed to tingle with a strange fire.

"I love you," the Duke said, "and I know I have a great deal to teach you about love, but, my precious, lovely, beautiful little wife, I have no wish to frighten you."

"How . . . could I be . . . frightened by . . . Apollo?" Lynda asked. "But . . . I did not . . . know that . . . love would be so . . . wonderful . . . or that it would burn inside me . . . like a fire."

"That is how I have been feeling for a long time," the Duke said, "and it is the sacred fire which comes from the Gods and which unites us with them."

Then he was kissing her again, and she knew he was carrying her up in the sky, and past the stars, to the Milky Way.

The Light of Apollo was burning within them.

As they became one, the ecstasy of their love swept them into a special Heaven known only to the Gods themselves.

ABOUT THE AUTHOR

Barbara Cartland, the world's most famous romantic novelist, who is also an historian, playwright, lecturer, political speaker and television personality, has now written over 593 books and sold over six hundred and twenty million copies all over the world.

She has also had many historical works published and has written four autobiographies as well as the biographies of her mother and that of her brother, Ronald Cartland, who was the first Member of Parliament to be killed in the last war. This book has a preface by Sir Winston Churchill and has just been republished with an introduction by Sir Arthur Bryant.

Love at the Helm, a novel written with the help and inspiration of the late Earl

Mountbatten of Burma, Great Uncle of His Royal Highness, The Prince of Wales, is being sold for the Mountbatten Memorial Trust.

She has broken the world record for the last sixteen years by writing an average of twenty-three books a year. In the *Guinness Book of World Records* she is listed as the world's top-selling author.

Miss Cartland in 1987 sang an Album of Love Songs with the Royal Philharmonic Orchestra.

In private life Barbara Cartland, who is a Dame of the Order of St. John of Jerusalem and Chairman of the St. John Council in Hertfordshire, has fought for better conditions and salaries for Midwives and Nurses.

She championed the cause for the Elderly in 1956, invoking a Government Enquiry into the "Housing Condition of Old People."

In 1962 she had the Law of England changed so that Local Authorities had to provide camps for their own Gypsies. This has meant that since then thousands and thousands of Gypsy children have been able to go to School, which they had never been able to do in the past, as their caravans were moved every twenty-four hours by the Police.

There are now fifteen camps in Hertfordshire and Barbara Cartland has her own Romany Gypsy Camp called "Barbaraville" by the Gypsies.

Her designs "Decorating with Love" are being sold all over the U.S.A. and the National Home

Fashions League made her, in 1981, "Woman of Achievement."

She is unique in that she was one and two in the Dalton list of Best Sellers, and one week had four books in the top twenty.

Barbara Cartland's book *Getting Older, Growing Younger* has been published in Great Britain and the U.S.A. and her fifth cookery book, *The Romance of Food*, is now being used by the House of Commons.

In 1984 she received at Kennedy Airport America's Bishop Wright Air Industry Award for her contribution to the development of aviation. In 1931 she and two R.A.F. Officers thought of, and carried, the first aeroplane-towed glider airmail.

During the War she was Chief Lady Welfare Officer in Bedfordshire, looking after 20,000 Servicemen and -women. She thought of having a pool of Wedding Dresses at the War Office so a Service Bride could hire a gown for the day.

She bought 1,000 gowns without coupons for the A.T.S., the W.A.A.F.'s and the W.R.E.N.S. In 1945 Barbara Cartland received the Certificate of Merit from Eastern Command.

In 1964 Barbara Cartland founded the National Association for Health of which she is the President, as a front for all the Health Stores and for any product made as alternative medicine.

This is now a £65 million turnover a year, with one-third going in export.

In January 1968 she received *La Médille de Vermeil de la Ville de Paris*. This is the highest award to be given in France by the City of Paris. She has sold 30 million books in France.

In March 1988 Barbara Cartland was asked by the Indian Government to open their Health Resort outside Delhi. This is almost the largest Health Resort in the world.

Barbara Cartland was received with great enthusiasm by her fans, who feted her at a reception in the City, and she received the gift of an embossed plate from the Government.

Barbara Cartland was made a Dame of the Order of the British Empire in the 1991 New Year's Honours List by Her Majesty, The Queen, for her contribution to Literature and also for her years of work for the community.

Dame Barbara has now written 593 books, the greatest number by a British author, passing the 564 books written by John Creasey.

AWARDS

1945 Received Certificate of Merit, Eastern
      Command, for being Welfare Officer to
      5,000 troops in Bedfordshire.
1953 Made a Commander of the Order of St.
      John of Jerusalem. Invested by H.R.H.
      The Duke of Gloucester at Buckingham
      Palace.
1972 Invested as Dame of Grace of the Order
      of St. John in London by The Lord Prior,
      Lord Cacia.
1981 Received "Achiever of the Year" from the
      National Home Furnishing Association
      in Colorado Springs, U.S.A., for her
      designs for wallpaper and fabrics.
1984 Received Bishop Wright Air Industry
      Award at Kennedy Airport, for inventing
      the aeroplane-towed Glider.
1988 Received from Monsieur Chirac, The
      Prime Minister, The Gold Medal of the
      City of Paris, at the Hotel de la Ville,
      Paris, for selling 25 million books and
      giving a lot of employment.
1991 Invested as Dame of the Order of The
      British Empire, by H.M. The Queen at
      Buckingham Palace for her contribution
      to Literature.

Called after her own beloved Camfield Place, each Camfield Novel of Love by Barbara Cartland is a thrilling, never-before published love story by the greatest romance writer of all time.

Barbara Cartland

___A CORONATION OF LOVE #107	0-515-10883-9/$3.50
___A WISH COMES TRUE #108	0-515-10904-5/$3.50
___LOVED FOR HIMSELF #109	0-515-10932-0/$3.99
___A KISS IN ROME #110	0-515-10958-4/$3.99
___HIDDEN BY LOVE #111	0-515-10983-5/$3.99
___THE PEAKS OF ECSTASY #116	0-515-11085-X/$3.99
___LUCKY LOGAN FINDS LOVE #117	0-515-11106-6/$3.99
___THE ANGEL AND THE RAKE #118	0-515-11122-8/$3.99
___THE QUEEN OF HEARTS #119	0-515-11139-2/$3.99
___THE WICKED WIDOW #120	0-515-11169-4/$3.99
___LOVE AT THE RITZ #122	0-515-11219-4/$3.99
___THE DANGEROUS MARRIAGE #123	0-515-11241-0/$3.99
___GOOD OR BAD #124	0-515-11258-5/$3.99
___THIS IS LOVE #125	0-515-11286-0/$3.99
___RUNNING AWAY TO LOVE #126	0-515-11316-6/$3.99
___LOOK WITH THE HEART #127	0-515-11341-7/$3.99
___SAFE IN PARADISE #128	0-515-11359-X/$3.99
___THE DUKE FINDS LOVE #129	0-515-11378-6/$3.99
___THE WONDERFUL DREAM #130 (June)	0-515-11394-8/$3.99

Payable in U.S. funds. No cash orders accepted. Postage & handling: $1.75 for one book, 75¢ for each additional. Maximum postage $5.50. Prices, postage and handling charges may change without notice. Visa, Amex, MasterCard call 1-800-788-6262, ext. 1, refer to ad # 211b

Or, check above books and send this order form to:	Bill my: ☐ Visa ☐ MasterCard ☐ Amex	
The Berkley Publishing Group 390 Murray Hill Pkwy., Dept. B East Rutherford, NJ 07073	Card#_____	(expires)
		($15 minimum)
	Signature_____	
Please allow 6 weeks for delivery.	Or enclosed is my: ☐ check ☐ money order	
Name_____	Book Total	$_____
Address_____	Postage & Handling	$_____
City_____	Applicable Sales Tax	$_____
State/ZIP_____	(NY, NJ, PA, CA, GST Can.) Total Amount Due	$_____